Erotic Collection 17

CJ EDWARDS

MMXIV

ISBN-13:
978-1511704298

ISBN-10:
1511704292

Acknowledgements

Cover Design by

Francessca's Romance Reviews

Proof reading by Kelsey Burns

With thanks.

CONTENTS

A Taste of India   5

Body Swap   17

Casting Coach   30

Santa Empties His   44
Sack

The Governor's Wife   55

The Nursing Mother   64

A Taste of India

"So what do you recommend, Jaz?" Del lounged back with his arm over the back of the restaurant seat as he openly ogled the petite Indian waitress. Jazwinder was no more than five foot four and her starched white blouse was stretched over a very tidy little body. No more than nineteen, she spoke excellent English but with a very pronounced Indian accent. Del and Sue reckoned she was a Birmingham native but had spent much of her childhood in India. Either way, she was the tastiest thing in the restaurant and Del wanted to fuck her so much his balls were aching.

Jaz shuffled from foot to foot as she recommended a Biryani and struggled to keep her composure as she felt her brown face burning. The older white man was very handsome and the couple radiated a sexuality she had never encountered before. She was an Indian born, UK raised Hindu with a strict, traditional family and as such was very naïve.

"What do you think love?" Del asked his wife as the tight buttocks moved provocatively away from them.

"I think you are a very bad man, my darling, but as usual, you have impeccable taste." Del and Sue had been in an open marriage for over ten of their fifteen years together and had shared some incredibly erotic experiences. By now they were expert seducers and had perfected a system between them that usually got them what and whom they wanted. They ate their curry slowly and took every opportunity to engage their server in conversation; learning a little more about her each time.

The end of the meal came all too fast and Jaz sashayed up to their table with the bill. She seemed expectant but most likely thought she was about to see the couple for the last time and was just exercising her flirting muscles. Del paid in cash and then slid a £50 note into the payment wallet and flashed her his best smile as the couple left. Jaz saw the red note from across the restaurant and went straight across to retrieve it. That was a lot of money for a single tip. She picked up the wallet and a card fell out with the money. It was blank and just had a handwritten message in Sue's elegant writing.

We like you a lot Jaz and would love to get to know you better. Give us a call.

There was a mobile number printed on the reverse. Jaz picked it up, thought for a moment and quickly walked into the back of her father's restaurant, telling her sister to cover her tables for a moment.

Del and Sue were sat in their Mercedes in the restaurant car park, waiting for the phone to ring. It was the wife who answered. "Hello Jaz," she said before the girl could speak.

"How did you know it was me?" the Indian stuttered.

Sue laughed but in a friendly way. "We're not taking you for granted my darling," she purred. "There was such a connection between us that we just knew you would call." She paused for just a moment. "My husband's gorgeous isn't he?" she added.

Jaz was struck dumb for a moment. She didn't really know why she had been so tempted to make the call but Sue clearly did. She fancied the older woman's husband and the wife didn't seem to mind. When she did find her voice, she was stammering. "I didn't mean, I mean, that is…!"

Sue quickly put her out of her misery. "Hey, don't worry. We both like you and we don't bite!" They both laughed together for long few seconds before the older woman moved things on. "So, do you want to party with us after work Jaz? We're right outside or can come back and pick you up."

The young woman was sorely tempted to just jump in the

car and throw caution to the wind but there was no way her dad would miss her absence and she told Sue as much.

"Not to worry," Sue told her quickly. "Are you off tomorrow afternoon?"

"Yes!"

"We'll send a car. Where shall we pick you up from?"

The arrangements were quickly made for a rendezvous in a 'safe' place. Jaz then quickly rang off and hurried back to work, wondering what the hell had just happened.

Del kissed his wife as she dropped her iPhone into the centre console of the car. "I am going to fuck her little brains out. I'm so hard for her."

Sue reached down and caressed her husband's bulging crotch. "Yes you are my stud," she whispered, "but if I let you loose on the poor little virgin in this condition, you'll destroy her. You let me run things. Okay?"

Del slid his hand into his wife's blouse and found a nipple to tweak. "You're the boss sweetheart," he told her. "Now let's go home so I can fuck *your* brains out!"

"My brains are always available for you to fuck them out," Sue smiled. "Will you be a good boy and fuck my arse tonight?"

Del left a thick layer of rubber on the tarmac as he screeched out of the car park.

Del and Sue were *not short of a few bob*, as Del liked to put it. The fact is, since a major international had bought the patent for his car tracking system, their lifestyle had gone from comfortable to ridiculously stinking rich. They lived in a huge house on the edge of town and had just about everything they ever wanted. With one exception! Sue longed for children but years of tests had found her to be completely barren. So they filled the gap with fun, games and debauchery. Jaz was about to become their latest toy.

The car they sent was designed to be ostentatious and the driver fitted the bill perfectly. Ex-soldier Jeff had worked for the couple for over two years as chauffeur, handyman, sometime bodyguard and regular stud. He was six foot of muscle and kept his thirty five year old body in prime condition in the house gym while he waited for his employers to call on his services. Or more specifically, Sue!

The meeting place was a bus stop in the Hall Green area of

Birmingham. Jaz chose it because it was easy to get to, her family had no connections there and there was enough of an Indian population that she wouldn't draw attention; a pretty young Hindu girl in a sari. She just got off one bus and stood at the stop as though she was waiting for another.

When the car drew up, Jaz didn't move as she assumed it was just pulling over for some other reason. Even though she was expecting a car to pick her up at that time, she couldn't make the mental leap to associate the twenty foot limousine with the offhand 'we'll send a car for you' comment of Sue's. The huge, smartly dressed white man who got out of the driving seat wasn't taking no for an answer though. Opening the door, he scooped her into back and was pulling away from the curb before she knew what was happening.

The inside of the car was sumptuous. Plush seats faced each other, with plenty of legroom between and other luxuries, such as a TV and a minibar. The dark glass between front and rear opened silently and Jaz heard the deep, rumbling tones of the driver. "Help yourself to drinks Jaz. We've got most things in there."

"I don't drink thank you," she answered automatically.

"Go on," the man urged. "It'll help you relax. Besides," he chuckled as the window closed. "I have a feeling today is going to a day of firsts for you." Jaz cracked open an alcoholic fruit juice without another thought and pondered over his words as she tasted her very first grown up drink.

The young woman was on her second as the car turned into a sweeping drive and crunched to a gravelly halt outside an imposing front entrance. Her door was opened and she knocked back the rest of her drink before climbing out on surprisingly unsteady legs. "This way," Jeff said kindly and took her arm to guide her indoors, rather than running the risk of her falling flat on her face when climbing the stone steps. They walked through a grand hallway and up a grand staircase; only pausing for a moment in front of double doors at the top, before Jeff through them open and led her inside.

Jaz took a split second to take in at the sights and sounds within and nearly fell over. Del was standing in the middle of a bedroom floor with his suit trousers around his ankles and his wife was kneeling in front of him. She was completely topless; her magnificent tits bared to the girl's sight and her husband's cock buried in her throat. The innocent Indian found her legs, turned quickly and ran straight into a wall of muscle. "Come on." Jeff said kindly, as he guided her to a soft chair that was no more than a foot from the action. "Your hosts don't want you to leave already."

Sue let her husband's cock slip from her mouth and gently massaged it with her hand as she spoke. "That's right my darling. This is your sex education class. Make the most of it!" She held the fat cock in her hand up for the other woman to see. "Magnificent isn't he?"

"Umm, yes. I am guessing so," Jaz muttered, feeling her face burning and other, less understandable sensations throughout her body. She was not to know that the alcopops in the car, like all of the drinks, were liberally laced with Spanish Fly which was having a profound effect on her.

An experienced seducer like Sue didn't miss a thing. She saw the girl's wide pupils and heavy breathing. She also couldn't miss the rock hard nipples that were pushing up the material of her sari or the little, involuntary movements of her hips. She extended a finger and slowly crooked it in an exaggerated beckoning motion. "Come here, Jaz," she commanded in a soft but firm voice. Jaz got up unsteadily and took the few steps to Del's side. Sue then reached up to take her hand and the girl found herself on her knees, face to cock with the man of the house. "Go on," Sue continued. "Touch it! It doesn't bite!"

Jaz reached out her hand and lightly touched a finger to the glans of Del's cock as though taking its pulse and indeed she could feel a heartbeat through her fingertips. "It's so soft," she exclaimed.

Sue just sat back and watched fascinated as the little Indian girl explored her husband's sex organ. Her hand gently closed around the shaft and made a startling contrast of colours which the older woman found oddly arousing. In that moment she decided that she had to see her husband ride the girl and would do whatever was necessary to ensure she didn't leave with her hymen. Jaz began to instinctively run her hand up and down the shaft and judging by the encouraging noises coming from Del, she was doing it right.

In due course, Jaz was properly wanking her husband and Sue decided it was time to up the ante. "He wants you to kiss him now," she said softly, with her hand on the back of the girl's head, softly caressing her hair. "Go on," she encouraged, gently but firmly easing her face towards the end of Del's cock.

When the Indian girl's soft brown lips connected with the rubbery tip of the white man's glans, she jumped back, as though getting an electric shock; apparently surprised by the texture. "Come on girl," Sue cajoled her; pushing harder on her head and propelling her forward fast then Jaz was expecting. Her mouth was still slightly open and that was just enough for the fat cock to pop inside.

Jaz clearly liked sucking cock but she performed as an enthusiastic amateur, pumping her hand up and down and showing a distinct lack of coordination between hand and mouth. Sue watched her for a while before intervening. "How does that feel darling?" She asked her husband.

Del had a hand on top of the girl's soft, brown hair. "She's got a lovely soft, hot little mouth honey," he told her. "But she needs a bit of guidance."

Sue moved a little closer and pulled Jaz back so the cock dropped from her mouth. "Watch how a slut sucks cock," she told her. She put her arms behind her back and clasped them together, nuzzling at the cock with her face until she could catch in in her mouth. She pushed forward and swallowed the entire eight inches in one. Jaz caught her breath and her eyes looked like they were going to pop out of her head in disbelief at what she was watching. Her wonder just increased as the older woman bobbed back and forth, swallowing the entire meat sword into her throat each time without missing a beat.

Sue demonstrated for a few minutes before letting her husband fall from her mouth. "The man wants to see complete submission from you when you suck him," she explained to her eager pupil. "That's a big part of the stimulation for him and very important to Dominants like my husband." She held the cock in Jaz's direction again. "Ready to try?"

Jaz moved across on her knees and Sue settled in behind her; pressing her ample boobs into the girl's back and pressing her cheek against Jaz's from behind. "Let's do this together," she murmured. "A joint blow job!"

This time when Jaz parted her plump brown lips to receive Del, Sue was right there with her, so close she could inhale her husband's musky scent as he started Jaz's debasement. Pulling back was no longer an option for the naïve girl. Sue's body was hot and firm against hers and it would be her controlling the show. The older woman's hands closed on her forearms and drew them back behind her back again, trapped between their two bodies and pressing against Sue's tits. Sue then returned her hands to Jaz's waist.

Del started slow and easy to let the girl think she was controlling the action. He didn't want to scare her at this early stage. All the same, there would be no doubt soon. He always ended up face fucking his woman before he came. He gently took the young woman's hair in both his hands and slowly worked his cock into her throat.

Jaz panicked just once as the thick meat blocked her throat but the calming presence of her mentor helped her through it. Sue saw the moment coming and gently stroked her cheek to help her through it, holding her in place just long enough and then releasing the pressure so she could pull back and suck in some air around the cock. Pretty soon she was bobbing back and forwards like a pro.

Once she saw that Jaz was lost in her rhythm, Sue began to warm her up for her inevitable fucking. Her hands subtly snaked up from the girl's waist and found her breasts, gently stroking and kneading them through the sari material. Far from pulling away from these female advances, Jaz seemed to melt into her hand, whether subconsciously or otherwise. Sue took this as a green light and moved one hand and then the other up to the Indian's shoulder to unfasten the sari and work it downwards.

Jaz didn't seem to notice her clothes coming off, she was pumping her head back and forth fast by now; the big cock hit the back of her throat with each entrance and extracting a curious *glug* from the girl, punctuated by muted little cries that were making Sue's panties damp. She wore a little sort of blouse under the sari that was soon unbuttoned and wrenched down her arms and then there was just the bra. Looking up at her husband to exchange a knowing look, she watched him take Jaz's head in a firmer grip and then quickly unclipped the garment and whipped it off.

Predictably, Jaz began to struggle, trying to pull away but she had no chance. Del kept hold of her head and lodged his prick deep in her throat while Sue's hands came back around and cupped the firm brown tits, squeezing the flesh and working the rubbery nipples between her fingers. "Your tits are so lovely," she purred. "I could play with them all day." Jaz continued to struggle and Del kept her airway blocked until she relaxed again and all this time Sue was purring in her ear, telling her to take it easy and enjoy the sensations as she enjoyed the girl's breasts and pretty soon the combined stimulation had the desired effect; as did the aphrodisiac still in her system.

As her husband stepped up the pace and began to face fuck the hapless girl, Sue's hands really began to roam. Slipping into a big pair of cotton pants, she tugged gently at the big curls within before seeking a very moist slit. Gently dipping a finger inside, she enjoyed the feel of the soft virgin flesh as she gently finger fucked her.

Jaz was completely zoned out. The big, strong cock was hammering in and out of her mouth as she seemed to have learned to automatically breathe around it. In the meantime, the fingers on her body were making her so... hot! She was lost to her emotions and didn't recognise the warning signs of Del's impending ejaculation. Sue did of course and didn't want Del's spunk spewed out across her carpet. She had a much better use for it. Continuing her coaching, she whispered in the girl's ear. "Here he comes, get ready. Swallow what you must and leave the rest in your mouth. Come on, concentrate," she pinched a thick chocolaty nipple for emphasis.

Del was a heavy cummer, he always had been. Gripping Jaz's head firmly, he rammed himself deep into her throat and his cock twitched as his balls emptied into that welcome cavern. Once, twice, three times and more. Wad after wad flew out of the end of his cock and filled the girl up.

Jaz looked a mess. Her make-up had run and cum was dribbling from the corner of her mouth but that mouth was at least full. Sue got to her feet and pulled the girl up with her, immediately smashing their lips together. Jaz didn't react at all, she was in shock.

Sue literally licked her husband's sperm from her slut's

mouth, an action that soon turned into a full on snog. The remainder of the girl's clothes were quickly discarded and her body responded to the woman's every touch.

Eventually Sue broke away and looked into the young woman's deep brown eyes. Eyes which were misty and lacked focus. "I'm going to make love to you now darling," she said simply, leading her by the hand towards the bed.

"I'm not a lesbian you know," Jaz replied, without conviction.

"Do you think I am?" Sue replied with heavy sarcasm in her voice. "Do you think I would ever give this up?" She grabbed her husband's flaccid cock as she passed him, giving it a little squeeze. "Don't worry about a thing," she said in a more loving tone." I'm going to make you feel wonderful." They reached the bed and Sue helped a willing Jaz on to her back, spread her legs nice and wide and lowered her head towards that tangled jungle of black hair.

Jaz was soon completely lost to her passion as Sue experienced tongue and fingers turned her inside out. Her first orgasm took her completely by surprise. She had of course come before – she had a vibrator. This wasn't it though. It built slowly and surely to take control of her whole body like a rolling tsunami. Her pussy buzzed and quivered, her legs began to shake and her body twitched. Then it hit her brain and she went berserk. "Oh! Oh! Oh! Oh! Oh Dear! Oh God! Ohhhhhhhh!"

Sue climbed off the still shaking young woman and nodded to her husband, who was admirably hard again after that girl on girl show. "She's all yours lover," she smiled. Del climbed between the slender thighs and positioned his heavy glans against Jaz's very sloppy cunt. Girding his loins, he slapped the groggy girl's cheek to get her attention. "This is where I make a woman of you, little one," he told her.

"God no," Jaz shrieked. "I can't do that. You can't have me. My dad. He will kill me!"

Sue was at her side. "Your dad won't know kitten! Just relax, he won't hurt you."

"But I'm to be intact. My dad has arranged a marriage…!"

"Forget about your dad and his pervy cousins," Sue continued. "This is for you!" That was a lie of course. It was mostly for Del and Sue. She nodded to Del and he began to ease inside a very tight passage as Sue held the girl's hand.

This was some deflowering for Del and Sue! The girl was innocent, so smoulderingly sexy and so fresh, so tight, but she still had some doubts. "Please don't," she begged. "We must be virgin to marry in my culture. My father will disown me!"

Sue bent over and kissed the girl on the lips. "If your father disowns you, then we will own you my little flower. You are so sexy, I know you want this."

"Hey, your people wrote the Karma Sutra after all," Del chipped in, still making tantalising little circles with his cock just inside her.

"Let's write another chapter," laughed Sue.

The time for talk was over. Del reached over and found the pert, brown tits with his big hands, pulling on the pointy nipples as he pushed his cock into her.

"Oh God, it hurts!" Jaz groaned. She could feel centimetre of her cervix stretching as this thick invader entered her.

"Not for long kitten," Sue soothed. "Bear with it. It's worth it!"

After easing half of his length inside, Del suddenly stopped. "There it is," he exclaimed, excitement in his voice. Sue squeezed the girl's hand again and watched her face avidly. She didn't want to miss this.

Suddenly, with a violent thrust of his powerful hips, Del exploded his way through the girl's maidenhead. There was a pause that seemed to last for ever but in reality was only a fraction of a second and then Jaz let out a mournful cry that seemed to come from the very centre of her being. "Ooooooooooh!" There was something in that cry that charged the air. Del's cock twitched, as did Sue's pussy. And then the fucking really started.

Del reached for the girl's shoulders to pull her tight quim on to his cock. Even with the copious amount of fluid leaking from her, she was still painfully tight. His muscular rump acted like a battering ram to force entry, again and again, pushing erotic little cries from the Hindi girl. "Ai! Ai! Ai!"

The scene was so intensely sensual that Sue had to reach for her own pussy as she watched her fit husband's white arse pump up and down, with the slender brown legs draped across it.

As she watched the emotions fly across Jazwinder's innocent face; fear, confusion, discomfort; excitement; arousal. As she watched the violent movements that Del started telegraphed through the slender brown body and converted to rare pleasure. All that was too much for the sexual creature. She lay back next to the couple, ripped her own clothes off and began to thrust her fingers inside her.

As Sue rapidly reached her own conclusion, she looked across to see her husband about to finish inside Jaz. "Christ," she moaned. "Don't knock her up. Not at this stage! Put it in me!"

Without missing a beat, Del withdrew from a very disappointed Jaz and slipped straight into his wife. It took maybe another ten thrusts, no more and he pumped a huge load inside her. Far more than she had taken from him before.

Sue lay back as Del pulled out. She was sated but had yet to come. She looked across at Jaz, who had a dreamy look on her face. "I believe you owe me one, chicken," she whispered.

There was no coercion, no compulsion. Jaz rolled off the bed and on to her knees, landing between the older woman's legs. Without any hesitation, she dipped her head and lapped at the jism dribbling from Sue's shaven slit.

The little Indian girl was either a quick learner or had a natural talent. Her long tongue traced a path from Sue's puckered anus to her throbbing button, dipping deep inside her open slit to collect the combined juices. Del stepped back and watched his own Karma Sutra page coming to life. He had a thought. "I've gotta get this on camera!" Leaving the room for a moment, he was soon back with his HD compact.

Sue was a sexual creature, she rarely went a day without several sessions. She had had men, women, boys and girls. One at a time to full-blown gangbangs. This girl was something special though, she decided. As the clever tongue continued to turn her inside out, the small brown hands were busy too, running up and down her body; clit to nipples.

It was never going to last long and when Sue blew it was volcanic in proportions. "Oh my fucking God! Yeeeees!" She bucked her powerful hips so hard that Jaz was tossed across the floor but it didn't matter, there was enough energy stored inside that orgasm to just keep on going. Oh fuck! Oh fuck! Oh fuck!"

15

The other two just watched as the elegant woman lost all her dignity and convulsed like a woman possessed.

When Sue recovered at least some of her senses, she found Jaz snuggled in beside her. Putting a protective arm around her, she gently stroked her soft black hair. "That was just incredible," she breathed. "Where did you learn that?"

Jaz was drowsy with slumber; almost asleep but she managed to raise her head. "I was always a keen reader," she smiled.

"And which book taught you cunnilingus?"

"The Karma Sutra of course!"

Sue looked at her husband. "Oh my God! We've got to keep her!"

Body Swap

"Of course, you could always do one of those body swaps…" Dana had zoned out of her bestie's beauty monologue ages ago but that statement dragged her straight back into the room. The busy media scheduler had let her lifelong weight problem catch up with her in recent years. Always pretty, the forty three year old's pretty, ageless reflection stared back at her in a fleshy surround.

Lia was generally full of crap but she knew her beauty and she knew her tech. That was her life after all. Dana watched the platinum blonde recline on her chair as she sipped at her ice coffee. She knew she had her and was relishing the moment. She couldn't resist taking the bait any longer. "Yeah, well the body swapping's all about the rich and famous," she answered; trying to sound disinterested and failing. "It's about jumping into your partner's body for sex and other kinky stuff. Right?"

Lia giggled like the school girl she resembled after her latest improvements. "Wrong, honey. You're about fifty years behind the times. It is 2115 you know!"

"And what are you telling me?"

"The big users are the PTs," she replied smugly. "Personal trainers," she added. Just in case her fat friend didn't know what they were. "Their customers are mostly not the rich and famous. They're already perfect." She sipped her drink again and drank in

17

the moment. "Their customers are pretty but overweight media schedulers with good credit and bad willpower." She sat back and didn't even try not to look smug.

"And?"

"And they will set you up on a payment plan to body swap for as long as it takes to get your fat arse back in the habit of going to the gym!"

Dana slugged back her own flavour packed cold drink. "That's horse crap," she told her friend.

"But you'll look into it," Lia answered. "I know you!"

"Of course," Dana called over her shoulder; already halfway through the café door. "You know me...!"

And three weeks later, Dana was sat in front of the most gorgeous woman she had ever set eyes on to discuss body swap. Houston was a personal trainer of some considerable experience and Dana had no idea how old she was. Her face was completely lineless and her skin flawless. The oval shape and soft cheeks were those of a teenager but her eyes were older; far older. Her hair was straight and shoulder length; shimmering with health and vitality. And her body! There was nothing where it shouldn't be. Her breasts were the perfect size and shape, her midriff positively wasp like and her legs went on forever. And when she moved it was in such a sensual, sexy way, Dana's eyes were drawn moth-like to her. *What she could achieve if she looked like that...!*

"Did you follow all that?" Houston smiled, almost as if she knew how distracted her potential client was.

"Er, I think so," Dana stuttered. "You can do a full body swap so you can basically burn my fat for me or you can just impose your personality on mine to bolster my willpower."

"You were listening then." Houston's laugh was a dirty one but very pleasant all the same. "I recommend two full swap sessions first, just so I can get your training into gear. Then I'll dip in and out as required to keep you going." She paused and focused her piercing blue eyes on the media scheduler. "You do appreciate the implications of our arrangement?"

Dana had thought long and hard about this one over the preceding weeks. "Total lack of privacy you mean?" her reply was instantaneous.

"For me as well," Houston added. "At least during the total

swap sessions..." She produced a tablet with a wordy document displayed. "This protects both of our interests," she said and passed it across.

It took Dana the best part of an hour to read. There were financial clauses to protect their assets and income; personal stuff covering subjects like no permanent body markings or piercings without prior permission; rules about interaction with each other's friends and intimates and so on. By the time she had finished, her head was spinning and she had downed several soft drinks that Houston had put in front of her without her asking for them. The last bit was the payment, which was affordable but painful. Dana took a deep breath and then pressed her thumb in the signature box. The deed was done! "When do we start?"

"No time like the present," Houston spoke absent-mindedly as she finished off the contract. "I've blocked off the rest of the afternoon for you." She poked the tablet screen to send the signed contract off to wherever it was going. "Come on," she beckoned. "I'll show you the office."

The office was no more than a cosy little room with easy chairs and a screen wall. "Make yourself comfortable," the trainer told her client. "I'll boot up."

Two minutes later and they were sitting side by side, looking at a kaleidoscope of moving shapes and listening to some soothing music. Houston explained that the show was to facilitate mediation, which just eased her into the process for the first time. It wasn't strictly necessary but most people found it helped. They both wore a light helmet on their heads, which contained all the equipment necessary for the transference. Houston just had to flick the switch. Dana closed her eyes and let the music take her.

"How was it for you?" Houston's voice seemed different somehow. As Dana floated back up the levels of consciousness and her vision returned, she saw straight away that something was different. She turned her head and almost jumped out of her skin to see her own face looking back at her. She was expecting it but it was still spooky as hell. Houston/Dana was studying her tablet again. "Perfect transference," she finally announced with a smug voice that wasn't hers.

It took a few minutes for Dana to find her feet, literally as well as figuratively and as she adjusted Houston bustled around in her overweight body, clearly far more accustomed to the process. "You brought your gym kit didn't you?" The personal trainer was already on her way out the door, full of enthusiasm at the idea of training another out of shape body.

"Sure, the bag's by the door," Dana told her, settling into a form-fitting easy seat in the lounge area.

"I'll let you find your own way around," Houston opened the door. "Obviously all the apartment settings will work for you; you are effectively me! Back in two hours," she added and then was gone.

Dana waited patiently until the monitor showed her host's vehicle had left the garage and then positively leapt out of her seat. She couldn't wait to have a look at her temporary body! Darting into Houston's bedroom, she activated the full length reflector panel and watched herself avidly as she slowly peeled the trainer's clothes off. Her skin was slightly tanned and completely flawless. Dana felt an odd shiver of excitement as she opened the blouse top and revealed the taut, bronzed flesh of her trainer's breasts. She reached a hand in and gently caressed the small pointy nipples. "Oh God!" It was Houston's voice but her own utterances. Unlike just about everyone she knew, Dana had never had a same sex relationship as she had bizarrely never found other women attractive. Something about this one and the complete control she had over her body for a limited period of time was however different. She couldn't help herself! She touched the breasts again and enjoyed the sensations. It was exactly like touching herself but more... alive! If this was what a super-fit body gave you, she wanted more of it. She wanted a lot more.

But first she wanted this particular body. She just had to fuck herself as Houston. Sitting on the bed, she squeezed the firm boobs together and then ran her fingers down the rock hard abs to the waxed mound below. With a satisfied moan, she lay back and let her practiced hands do their thing.

****

Houston had just entered the gym foyer as her wrist alarm went. Glancing at the screen, she smiled inwardly at the image of herself lying back on her bed and pleasuring herself. The apartment brain would record the scene for her enjoyment later. In the meantime, she had a chubby body to whip into shape. Entering her code into the receptionist, as it of course didn't recognise her chit, she changed into the very baggy workout clothes she kept for this purpose and hit the machines. She really enjoyed this part of the job. She supposed she had become a pain junky, because working sedentary bodies at the intensity she was accustomed to was surely painful! After taking care to get a long warm up, she hit the machines like a woman possessed. This girl was going to ache some tomorrow! As her new curves rhythmically bounced in time with her exertions, she was very aware of all the interested sets of eyes that were glued to her.

Houston finished her long session with ten minutes in the massager and twenty in the sauna. Like most modern gyms, the steam room was mixed gender and clothing was forbidden, so it gave her the opportunity to flaunt Dana's curves properly for the same time and sure enough, she was soon deep in conversation with a man in his fifties.

"I've never seen you in here before. Why is that, I'm here every day?"

"I've finally decided to embrace the fitness lifestyle I guess." Dana's face smiled easily and Houston used it to her advantage.

"You're a very beautiful woman," The man's eyes dipped to her big juicy nipples that were now standing to attention like small penises. "I like my girls with a bit of meat on them. Not like all the other stick insects in here."

"Are you chatting me up?" Houston feigned innocence.

"Would you like me to, pretty lady?"

"Oh yes!"

Half an hour later, they were dressed and in his apartment, just around the corner. "Would you like some Champagne?" He waved a rare bottle of the real stuff in her direction.

"No. I would like some cock," the horny trainer threw back, enjoying the shocked look on the gentleman's face. Closing the gap between them, she sank to her knees and fished out his manhood. "Oh, that's a nice one," she said approvingly. Without further delay and very conscious of the ticking clock, she swallowed the seven inches right up to the root.

"Oh my goodness, that feels good," the silver fox moaned.

"You are something else."

Houston alternated between wanking him and sucking with the force of a vacuum cleaner, ensuring he was rock hard and firing on all cylinders before she tried out her new pussy. Leading him to his own bedroom, she pushed him back and quickly straddled him. When his cock pushed its way inside her, it felt so much tighter than she was used to. With a long moan, she steadied herself with her hands on his manly chest and began to ride with all the intensity she had shown in the gym.

In the twenty minutes Houston had left, she took two loads from the white haired man. After he had filled her once with his foamy cum, she quickly brought him back to life with her clever mouth and a practised manipulation of his prostrate. Once he was hard enough, she then offered him Dana's arse.

"Are you sure? Would you like me to find some lubricant?" He was enough of a gentleman to show concern.

"No," Houston snapped; as horny as hell. "I want it dry. Bugger me until I cry!"

No man could say no to the fleshy but firm buttocks that were waving enticingly in front of this lucky bloke. Taking a tight hold of her hips, he carefully lined himself up with her crinkled little hole and pushed for all he was worth.

It hurt even more than Houston anticipated. Anal was a regular thing for her and she was used to it going in easily. This hurt so much it actually burnt her insides. It clearly wasn't a regular thing at all. In fact, the trainer wondered if she was actually losing her anal cherry once more.

The nameless man soon got into his stride. Gripping her soft hips with a grip of iron, he buggered her uncompromisingly. The young woman, squirmed, moaned and bucked under his attention and that made it all the more exciting.

When he came, so did Houston. The intense sensations were different to what she was used to and threatened to overwhelm her. When the cock pulsed and she felt her insides being coated with warm, sticky spunk, it tipped her over. Her pussy buzzed and her arse bucked. "Oh my God! Yeeees!"

She quickly recovered and became business-like again, giving herself a quick clean and covering up. Leaving the man her own electronic details, she bustled outside and jumped back into her vehicle for the ten minute passage back to her place.

****

Dana had been having the time of her life. A bit of nosing around in the bedside drawers had revealed a whole host of pleasure toys; many she was familiar with and some she wasn't. Her first orgasm came just from her fingers and then she tried some electro-stimulation. Pretty soon she was writhing on the bed from the shocks penetrating her most sensitive zones: pussy, nipples and arsehole all rhythmically convulsing with sensations ranging from a little buzzing to full on shocks. She finished herself off with a good old fashioned dildo. Far bigger than she would normally be able to cope with, she took full advantage of Houston's more generous proportions down there, filling and stretching the trainer's flexible cunt.

She had lost count of how many times she had cum and was lying back recovering by time the transporter pulled up outside. Leaping up, she pulled on Houston's clothes and ran to activate the big screen, so she was lounging on a chair and watching an old movie when the door opened. "How was my workout?"

"Hard and fast," Houston chuckled. "You're gonna be sore later. Let's change shall we?"

Ten minutes later they were back in their own bodies. Dana worried whether Houston would be able to tell she had been pumping her pussy for the best part of two hours. Houston on the other hand had no doubt that Dana would be conscious of her throbbing arse and dripping twat. She arranged their next appointment and the older woman went back to her husband.

****

The next appointment was only two days later and the schedule dictated a similar scheme. Houston was to take Dana's body to the gym for another workout, while Dana waited for her again. The transfer was completed without delay and the trainer left her client behind in her body and her apartment once more.

This time, Dana resisted temptation and really did settle down to watch a film. The last time, her body had ached from joint and muscle and she intended to relax before she had to endure that. She found a romantic movie from the twentieth century and curled up on the sofa.

She only got half an hour her viewing when the door communicator sounded and made her jump out of her skin. She flicked over the channel on to the door camera and her chin dropped open. It was the most gorgeous man she had ever seen. "Come on darling," he called in an equally sexy voice. "I know you're in. Open up!"

Dana was in a bind. Although they hadn't discussed it, the two women has a contractual agreement not to interact with each other's family and friends. She had no idea who this man was but she reckoned he wasn't her brother. All the same, she couldn't just leave him there, knowing she was inside, or Houston, or whoever she was… Making an instant decision, she hit the entry button.

Antonio was a lot more desirable in the flesh. Dana met him in the doorway and he just fixed her for a moment with a smouldering look. "I thought you weren't gonna let up!"

"Yeah, well, I was in the bathroom…" Dana was very flustered and very much on the back foot, not knowing who this man was or what his intentions where. She tried to keep the nerves out of her voice but failed miserably.

"So, am I coming in?"

"Of course," Dana stepped back… And then the man pounced!

He grabbed her, pushed her against the wall hard enough to take her breath away and mashed his lips against hers. As he hungrily snogged her pliant lips, his hand wormed its way into her gym shorts and when he discovered she was panty free, his finger slipped straight inside her very wet pussy.

The hunk just fingered Houston/Dana for a few minutes as he pinned her against the hallway wall, letting her moan into his mouth. All of a sudden, he pulled away, releasing her mouth and cunt at the same time. He grabbed the front of her gym top with both hands and ripped it off her body with a loud ripping sound.

When her mouth was released for a moment, Dana started to protest, to tell him she wasn't Houston. And then she closed it

24

again. Why bother? That window of opportunity soon passed anyway as he pushed her to her knees so her eyes were level with a very prominent bulge.

Dana unfastened him and drew the angry cock out. She was staggered, it was enormous. So much so in fact that he must have been genetically enhanced. *Whatever!* It was magnificent and Dana had to have it. Closing her lips around the glans, which stretched her plump lips a little, she savoured the taste, the hardness and the vitality of the beast.

Dana was very used to fellating her husband but this was a lot different. She normally controlled the action with her hands and mouth but the mystery man was having none of this. Slapping her hands down, he grabbed her firmly by the head and began to thrust, as though fucking her cunt.

"Glug! Glug! Glug!" The thick cock plunged in and out of her throat, making her eyes water. Dana was unaccustomed to such brutal treatment but it seemed that Houston wasn't. Her airway accommodated the man easily as he face fucked her.

The blowjob wasn't to last long but Dana's pussy was dripping by time the big man reached down and scooped her into his arms. The destination was Houston's bedroom and he knew exactly where to find it of course. Kicking open the door, he dropped the girl on the bed and climbed straight on, between her spread thighs.

When he entered her, Dana thought it was the most glorious penetration she had ever experienced. He was huge but Houston seemed to be built to accommodate him; in that moment she wondered wryly what damage the man would do to her actual pussy. His toned arse flexed and his abdominal muscles flexed as he drove that rod of meat up inside her, so far she imagined she'd feel it the back of her throat again. Over and over, faster and faster, she was fucked harder than she had ever been and harder even than she thought possible.

They came together. Dana's pussy contracted hard as the man's cock spurted like a fire hose, leaving her dripping, sated and exhilarated. He wasn't stopping there though. Rolling off the bed, he started ferretting underneath it, clearly familiar with where Houston kept her things. "I'm gonna assume you still keep it here?"

He came up with a variety of leather and rubber straps and things that made Dana blanche. "What are you going to do with those?"

"What do I usually do with them?" His eyes laughed as he spoke. He rolled her on to her front and quickly fastened a combination strap to her neck and wrists, drawing her arms painfully up her back. "Plug or no plug?"

Dana said nothing. "Okay," he chuckled. "Plug it is." Parting her firm buttocks, he squirted some lube straight into the unsuspecting woman's back passage, making her scream at the sudden invasion of cold into her hot little crack.

"What are you doing?" Dana tried to keep her voice calm but she was terrified at the idea of ass-play. That was one thing she never even contemplated doing. The next thing she knew was an uncomfortable pressure as he pushed an improbably large butt plug against her little rosebud. *That sort of plug!*

Dana grunted as the hard rubber popped through her sphincter. It seemed that Houston was adapted amply behind as well. She wriggled her hips to help it seat properly and was just about used to it when a sudden movement in the corner of her eye alerted her to danger and her arse lit up with pain. "Arrrrgh!"

"That's a lot of noise," the man chuckled and Dana squinted behind her to see he had a serious looking whip in his hand. "Anyone would think you didn't love this shit," he added. He then gave her another one and another. Dana bit the pillow and tried to control her sobbing as the tears rolled down her face.

The whipping continued until Dana/Houston's arse was back and blue and striped all over. The whip went down and he pulled out the plug. "The best is yet to come Dana," he laughed as he climbed on to the backs of her thighs and lined up his heavy cock with her prepared arsehole.

Dana! He called her Dana! The penny dropped, just as he penetrated her in one long, hard, painful, exhilarating thrust. *The bastard knew she wasn't Houston!*

The buggering was hard and brutal for an anal virgin such as Dana. Houston's body was fully accustomed to it though and the discomfort was soon over, her body was soon awash with amazing sensations as the big cock rode her to orgasm again. When it hit her, it started in her arse and spread at the speed of light to capture her clitoris and then to the rest of her body. Her brain lit up in a kaleidoscope of colours and her hips bucked like a bronco, forcing her rider to hold on tight.

"I see you've met Antonio!" Dana slowly opened her eyes to find herself looking at her own face.

Confused for a moment, it took a few seconds for her to remember where she was and in whose body. "This wasn't an accident, was it?"

"Oh course not," laughed Houston/Dana. "As I was giving your body such a good workout, I thought it only fair for you to try mine out." She dropped her bag and began stripping her clothes off.

"Are you not going to help me up?" Dana was ready to go and quite keen to get her own skin back.

"You must be kidding," Houston laughed. "You think I'm gonna turn down the opportunity to fuck the best looking girl in town?" She climbed on the bed and, with Antonio's help, turned the exhausted woman on to her back.

Dana looked down past Houston's perfect tits to see the heady image of herself, in all her naked glory, crawling between her open thighs. The whole idea made her head spin. She collapsed down on the bed and lost herself to pleasure as Houston began to feed on her dripping wet pussy.

"Oh God!" The experienced woman hit the spot straight away. Dana had never tried lady sex before but she was immediately hooked. All of a sudden, she felt a desperate need to take this woman into her arms but of course she couldn't. They were strapped securely underneath her body. She looked up at Antonio. "Please let my arms go," she pleaded in a little girl voice.

Antonio didn't budge but Houston looked up from her pussy lapping. "Let her go, Antonio," she told him in school ma'am tones." The young man half rolled her and freed her arms in seconds, allowing Dana to reach down and stroke her own hair in a way that made Houston purr like a cat.

Without breaking her stride, Houston shuffled her body around and swung her leg over Dana's head, locking them into a sixty-nine. Then the passion really started.

The hairy pussy that was lowering itself over her face was intimidating for Dana to say the least. The fact that it was her own seemed to make it even scarier. All the same, as it closed over her mouth, it seemed the most natural thing in the world to reach up, grab the meaty bottom and drag the slimy cunny on to her tongue. The taste was unexpected. She wasn't sure really what to expect but it seemed to taste a lot like man cum. The thought flashed though her mind that Houston had just been fucked – in her body! She dismissed the idea and began to devour the pussy.

Antonio just stood back and idly rubbed his cock as he watched his girl and the woman in his girl's body frenetically fucking each other. They both appeared very hungry. Hips bucked and a duet of sweet moaning filled the air. His cock twitched in his hand as he looked forward to joining in.

Dana finished first. Maybe due to Houston's superior cunt-licking skills or perhaps because she was already highly tuned. All the same, her orgasm was impressive. Bucking those muscular personal trainer loins so hard that Houston had to hang on tight, she literally screamed with pleasure. "Oh yeeeeees!"

Houston's culmination was right behind. Her whole body rippled as she moaned into her own juicy pussy. She gathered herself quickly, rolled over and then back on to the other woman, so Dana was able to hold her in her arms as she lay back and spread her legs obscenely wide. "Come on lover," she called to Antonio. "I think it's about time you tried this pussy out!"

Antonio didn't need telling twice. Climbing on board, he held his big prick in one hand, as he spread the petals of that small pussy with the other. "Are you ready for this?"

"I'm always ready for your gorgeous cock," Houston winked. But she wasn't. As he eased his way inside her, she felt fuller than ever before, to the point she wondered if she was going to split. Turning her head to bury it in the shoulder of the other woman, she gave a mournful moan. "Ooooooh! Oh fuck that's tight!"

Antonio seized the woman's ample tits and squeezed as he rode her. Looking into the familiar eyes of his girl, over her shoulder, he rode the unfamiliar and very desirable body inhabited by Houston. Both women were clearly finding the experience very horny.

When Antonio blew his stack inside the woman on top of her, Dana was vaguely aware that it was her womb being blasted with vigorous sperm but oddly it didn't seem to bother her at all. Houston had come on her boyfriend's cock and Dana very nearly followed her into orgasm. She hugged her tightly and kissed her on the cheek. "Thank you," she whispered.

Houston jumped to her feet, still full of life, despite her exertions. She helped her client up and they walked through to the transfer room.

"You have a new boyfriend by the way," Houston's eyes twinkled in Dana's face as she flicked the switch.

Casting Couch

Sven reckoned he was a genius. A good looking divorcee with a high sex drive, he had always struggled to hold down a decent job and at forty five was finding it hard to move forward with his life. The lack of a proper career structure made it hard to pick up girls as well and for a while he was in real spiral. And then he hit gold dust.

After a final check of the eight cameras in the room, Sven sat back in his plush office chair and mused on the success he had had with this venture while he waited for the next girl to arrive. He had the gift of the gab, which is why he had always ended up in sales jobs. And this was the easiest sale in the world. He was good with cameras and had made a bit of a hobby of home movies, even doing some passable amateur sex films with his wife until she left him. He did keep them all and with a bit of crafty editing had no compunction about selling them to websites. Then he thought about starting a website of his own and once it was up, he needed material, which is when he had a Eureka moment.

London was full of gorgeous young women who wanted to make it in films. A few had very strict rules about what sort of films they would appear in but most would not. He placed a series of ads and when he was deluged with enquiries, bought and borrowed a load of camera equipment and rented a posh office for six weeks. Sven was a phoney casting agent!

It was only day one and Sven had already fucked two

students and a nurse. He checked his notes and saw that the next candidate was a bit older. She was a thirty three year old married mother and from her passport photo looked good. He was very conscious though that the camera could be too flattering and as he didn't fuck fat or ugly chicks, anyone who walked through the door that didn't meet his expectations would be turned straight away.

Finally a timid knock on the door. "Come in," he called. A young woman pushed the door open slowly and entered the office cautiously. Sven made up his mind instantly. This one would do; she wasn't leaving without a good load of his thick, creamy spunk dripping from her battered cunt. "Hello," he smiled. "You must be Gwendolen?"

"My friends call me Gwen," the slim MILF sang out in a Welsh valleys accent.

"Then it's definitely Gwen! Come in and have a seat on the sofa. Make yourself comfortable."

Sven watched the young woman carefully as she walked across the room. She was dressed as though attending a job interview in a silk blouse and A Line skirt; her dark, silky hair cascading on to her shoulders. He noted the movement of her tits against the silk and saw she had a good pair of top bollocks. Exactly how good, he would see very shortly. Once they were this far, they almost never backed out.

The whole process was long, involved and phoney. He advertised in Stage and the young women's gossip magazines for adult models and actresses and sent out detailed application forms to some of the thousands who responded to his email address. Over the course of a few weeks, he sifted out the ugly and boring to be left with the horny and hungry. He then spoke to the lucky few to invite them to a casting interview. Therefore, by the time they walked through that door, the young women were determined to do whatever it took to get their big break. They were ripe for being taken advantage of by someone like Sven and he wasn't about to disappoint.

Sven adjusted the camera sat in front of him and pointed out the others, before starting his questions. "Tell me something about yourself Gwen."

"Well, I'm thirty-three and married with a four year old

boy," she started.

"And why do you want to be in adult films?"

"Well, I want to be famous, I've heard it pays well and I like sex!"

"Fair enough," Sven smiled. She wasn't going to be disappointed on the last count, ,he thought. "What does your husband think of the idea of you having sex on camera?"

Gwen hesitated for a moment. "We haven't really discussed it but he'll be cool about it. He's very easy going," she added.

Sven almost laughed. He wondered how easy-going the guy would be if he saw his pretty little wife screaming his name as he rammed her with his horse-sized cock. That was the thing, even if his would-be film stars did have second thoughts, they certainly didn't after setting eyes on his manhood. He was really blessed in that department. "Okay," he grinned. "Let's run through how this thing works."

Gwen shuffled a little on the sticky leather couch and pulled her skirt down just enough to cover the backs of her slim thighs. She looked up expectantly like a schoolgirl waiting for her exam results as Sven began indeed to test her.

"Let me remind you how this works again Gwen," Sven started. "When you're ready, we are going to do a screen test and you are already being filmed." He pointed out all the cameras around the room. "I will edit your casting into a professional montage of your performance and send it to potential producers who may wish to hire you for between one and three thousand pounds an hour. How does that sound?"

"Fantastic," the young mum said enthusiastically. "What do I need to do?"

"We'll get there in a minute," Sven chuckled. "Would you like to earn one thousand or three thousand?"

"Three thousand of course," Gwen shot back light-heartedly.

"Well that depends really on three things: How you look, what you are prepared to do and how well you do it."

"Well, do I look all right?" Gwen asked playfully.

"Well, let's have a look. Would you please stand up and undress for me?"

This was the moment of truth. If they really were going to back out, it would be here! Of course she didn't. Gwen stood up a little clumsily, dropped her small handbag on to the floor and slowly began to unbutton her blouse.

"Keep looking into the camera darling," Sven coached her. "Think your very naughtiest thoughts at all times and communicate them to your viewers. Remember the sexiest thing that's ever happened to you and replay it in your head." Gwen let out a little giggle and bit the corner of her lip in a really horny schoolgirl sort of way that made Sven's cock rebound in his pants. "That's the idea," he chuckled.

When the blouse was open, Gwen slipped it off her arms and Sven held his breath. Her body was every bit as good as he'd hoped. Her belly was completely flat, with the slightest hint of a six-pack and the pretty, lacy bra bulged with a good sized bosom. He estimated a 36B but he didn't have to guess. "What's your bra size darling?"

"Thirty six B." *Bingo! He was so good at this shit!*

The skirt was peeled down next and when the yummy mummy reached down to unfasten her shoes, Sven stopped her. "Leave the shoes on. It's sexier that way!" She straightened up. "Your bra next," he encouraged her.

Gwen made a real show of that. Slowly reaching behind her, she worked all three of the catches one at a time and held the elastic straps in place with her upper arms for a full minute as she bent forward to tease both the camera and Sven with her jiggling globes. Sven made a mental note to really punish the bitch with his cock when he got the chance. When her arms dropped and the cups finally came away, it was well worth the wait. Her tits were just perfect! Golden skin stretched across firm but not too firm mammary flesh; fat but perky. Two long pink nipples pointed straight at the would-be caster like small boys penises. "You like?" Gwen could clearly see the reaction she was having on him.

"Oh, I like!" Sven agreed, trying to regain his professional demeanour. "Now your panties!" Gwen reached down and slowly peeled the delicate lace down her thighs, revealing a carefully pruned dark landing strip as richly dark as the hair on her head. Carefully easing them over her shoes, she then turned a full three hundred and sixty degrees as directed, with her hands above her head. "Walk over here," Sven beckoned her and when she stood by his chair, he fondled her delightful tits for a couple of minutes, ostensibly to check they were completely natural. "Very nice," he exclaimed eventually. "Now sit back down." The pretty Welsh girl sat back in exactly the same spot on the leather couch but this time had nothing between her skin and the shiny leather.

Sven sat back and looked at the naked housewife, sat patiently with her hands on her knees, which her together modestly. Gwen really was a wet dream and he couldn't wait to have his cock sheathed in her. But he had to be patient. There was a tried and tested formula to follow and it would be a real shame to ruin it at this late stage. "You seem very comfortable in front of the camera," he said. ""Have you done anything like this before?"

Gwen shuffled uncomfortably for a moment and Sven wondered if he had hit a nerve for a moment until she answered. "My husband has filmed me a few times. You know…!"

Sven couldn't help laughing. "You mean you've made amateur sex films? Perfect! You should be a natural at this." He zoomed the main camera in on the young woman's pretty face. "I'm going to ask you some specifics now," he continued. "Just to get an idea of what your potential is. Is that okay?"

"Sure," Gwen nodded her head in confirmation. "What do you want to know?"

"Okay then. First of all, would you have sex with another woman?"

"I think so, yes!"

"Have you done that before?"

"Yes!"

"Okay then. What about more than one man?"

"At the same time?"

"Er yes!"

"Yes. I could do that."

"Have you done it before?"

"No!"

"Anal?"

34

Gwen went quiet and looked at the floor. Once again, Sven saw there was a story there. This girl was easier to read than a book! "I tried it once and it hurt too much," she answered finally.

"It only hurts if you don't do it right," Sven assured her. "Would you be prepared to try it again with someone who knows what they're doing? It makes you far more employable," he added.

"Okay. Maybe!"

"How about BDSM?"

Gwen looked up again. "You mean tying up and stuff? Yeah, I've done a bit of that."

"Good." Sven zoomed the camera out a little to cover her pointy pink nipples as well as her face. "Let's make a start on things then, shall we? How often do you masturbate?"

"Er, two or three times a week!"

"And do you use your fingers or a toy?"

"Both!"

"Okay then. I'd like you to sit back and wank for the camera."

"Now?"

"Yes Gwen, right now!"

The young woman reclined back into the soft cushions of the leather sofa and lifted her heels up on to the seat; spreading her thighs wide and revealing the glistening pearl of her vagina. She was wide open and primed for sex. Her long middle finger pushed the hood of her clitoris to the side to reveal the bean in the centre and then she began to rub.

Gwen was a fast starter. She had hardly touched herself and was already fully aroused. Her firm tits rose and fell with her breathing and she began to make the cutest little noises. Sven couldn't miss any of that. He got up from behind the desk with his camera and walked across the room, focusing straight on her flowering twat.

"That's great sweetheart," Sven crooned. "Make love to the camera."

"Ahh! Yes. Oh God. Yeeeees!" Gwen's back arched and her hips bucked in several sharp, staccato movements as her pussy gave up it juice, all over her fingers.

"That's beautiful. Now lick it off your fingers," Sven urged. Gwen licked and sucked, never taking her eyes off the lens.

Sven gave her a minute to recover a little and then sat down next to her on the sofa. "That was a really good start Gwen," he told her. "You need to demonstrate that you can work with male talent though. Are you ready?" Gwen looked around expectantly in a fairly comical way. "Me Gwen," Sven asserted. "I'm the talent. Now, I need you to suck my cock. Is that alright?"

She turned her head and looked at him from the corner of her eye for a moment, apparently thinking. Then looked back at the camera lens. "Sure. Why not? Do you want me to... you know!"

"That's right Gwen. Unzip me and take my cock out!"

Gwen reached across, unzipped and put her hand in Sven's trousers. Then she froze.

"Go on. Take it out. I'm still filming!"

It took some effort on her part but the slight young mum managed to tug the monster out and she just couldn't keep the shock off her face. It was the biggest cock she had seen by a long, long chalk. Her fragile little hand barely closed around the shaft. She slowly rubbed it into life as she put out a small tongue to taste the salty tip.

"That's good," Sven urged. "Take me in your mouth!"

"Nggug!" Gwen gagged as soon as the tip was in, it was so thick her whole mouth was stretched wide open. Sven put his free hand on the back of her head and slowly eased her on to him until only two inches of his ten was visible outside.

What followed next was a full-on face-fucking and Sven got it all on camera for the internet later. Gwen gagged and spluttered before learning to breathe around the solid column of gristle that was reaming her throat out. She had the odd moment of panic that made great film but for the most part she was completely compliant and let the big second generation Russian just fuck her throat with his hefty dick.

"I'm coming," Sven announced. "Hold it in your mouth." He pulled back so just the tip was filling the pretty MILF's mouth again and wanked his cum inside.

It was a good mouthful but Gwen could cope with it. She dutifully opened her mouth for the camera and then swallowed down every drop.

"Not bad at all," Sven praised her. "Now go and bend over the desk." Gwen got up and faced the desk. Bending at the waist, with straight legs, she rested her boobs on the hand surface and wriggled her arse for the horny Russian.

Sven placed the camera in his hand back on the desk and instructed the pretty housewife to look back into the lens. He then dropped to his knees and began to noisily eat her sweet pussy out.

Gwen's face ran through a full compendium of emotions for the camera as the long and experienced tongue took her to heaven. She felt the petals of her vagina open and pulse as they filled with blood.

Her orgasm hit her hard. Gwen's hips bucked up and down and the big Russian had to hold her firmly in place to avoid being bucked off. He stood up and placed a hand on her slit to feel the heat. "You cum beautifully," he said. "That will make good film. Now stay exactly like that."

Gwen heard his clothes come off and then sensed his hard body up against her soft behind. "What do you think is going to happen now?"

Gwen looked back. "We're going to make love?"

"No!" Sven placed his resurgent cock against her hot pocket. "I'm gonna fuck you!" He flexed his hips and Gwen bit her lip as her inflamed pussy lips stretched to accommodate his girth.

The hot housewife considered herself well versed in lovemaking but the fucking Sven gave her was like nothing she had experienced before. The language he used inflamed her passion from the start and when that big fat cock wormed its way inside her oh so tight pussy tube, it lit a flame deep inside her that she knew would be difficult, if not impossible to extinguish. She felt his hammer-like helmet butt up against her cervix and knew there was still more of him to go. She felt his strong hands on her slim hips; thumbs reaching across to part her firm buttock cheeks and gaze into her dark crevice.

When his cock slowly drew out, he took her with him. Her

pussy was so tightly wrapped around his meat that it literally
turned itself inside out. Gwen exhaled with a tortured moan as
electricity danced over her clitoris. "Arrrrgh! Yes! Oh my
fucking God!"

Sven loved the reaction his giant had on unsuspecting
women. She was the first wife he had fucked for some time. His
usual prey was college girls. Even so, she was just as
unprepared for the cunt battering she was about to get as the
most virginal eighteen year old. "I'm gonna destroy your pretty
pussy," he whispered in her ear as he took a tighter hold of her
hips.

The office filled with a choir of sex noises. The *slap, slap,*
of Sven's hard body connecting with Gwen's soft buttocks
mixed with the horny little grunts she made as her love tube
continued to stretch and the little girl cries that indicted each
time he bottomed out.

Sven fully intended to pump the horny wife full of spunk
but he wanted to see her face as he did it, so reluctantly pulled
out and span her around. Her little quim was gaping open from
the ravages of his monster cock and once she was on her back
on the desk, thighs akimbo, it was no effort to slip back in. He
had her hold the camera herself to alternately film both her face
and the spectacle of his cock pumping her. He took her full
breasts in his big hands and used them to pull her body back
and forward, spearing her repeatedly on his cock. Her pretty
face was just a picture. She had a look of confusion playing
across the desire and discomfort. His cock really did reach the
parts that others couldn't reach.

She had come at least twice when Sven finally stiffened
and unloaded his balls into her. A moment of shock crossed her
face when she realised he was bareback and then a third orgasm
overtook her. "Ohhhhhhhh!"

Sven withdrew and held the camera up to her puffy red
pussy. "Hold your lips open and push the cum out," he
commanded. Gwen did her best and showed the world she had
been seeded by a man she had only met half an hour before.

"You did really well," Sven told her. "You can dress now."
As he watched Gwen pull her clothes back on he had a thought.
"I've got more than enough for a great casting tape for you but

would you like to improve your employability options?"

"How would I do that?" Gwen wondered who else she had to fuck to get a toehold in this industry but she'd made the first step and was adamant she was going to succeed.

Sven never saw these girls more than once but this one was such a great fuck, he fancied trying something clever. "There's a couple of tricks you haven't demonstrated yet," he smiled as he watched her fastening the last couple of buttons on her blouse. She looked great dressed as well and his cock was already beginning to stir again. The next girl of the afternoon was going to get a good fucking. "Can you come back in tomorrow at three?"

"Sure, why not?" Gwen smiled as though she had just made an arrangement to have her nails done or something and was gone. Sven wondered how she was going to handle being tied up and whipped before her first proper buggering. He took his resurgent cock in his hand and absent-mindedly rubbed it a couple of times. Then he realised he was naked and his next girl was due. He quickly pulled on his shirt and trousers just in time for another soft knock on the door.

Georgina was a timid little flower who didn't really know what she was getting into. A nursing student at the university and desperate to make some money, she had been persuaded by her friends to answer the ad. Sven ran through his normal question set and quickly realised she was very inexperienced. All the same, his blood was up after Gwen. He was going to really corrupt this girl.

The usual striptease for the camera revealed she was a true ginger and that got him curious. There was a theory he had read that redheads had a much higher pain threshold than other people and as he couldn't get the idea of thrashing Gwen's wriggling arse out of his head, he thought he'd try something different with this nervous teenager. He looked her up and down and admired the cute freckly face with its green eyes and snub nose, the slightly skinny frame with its apple-shaped tits and the womanly flare of its hips, around an uncultured red bush. He started his pitch. "There's lots of different ways you can sell yourself in this industry, Georgina, but my clients are looking for something in particular. Have you ever done light

BDSM?"

"I'm not really sure what that is to be honest Sir?"

Sir? Did she honestly just call him Sir when he mentioned BDSM! "Have you ever been spanked Georgina?"

The young woman blushed the colour of her hair. "No, not really, I mean no!"

"You don't seem very sure... You can earn up to five thousand pound an hour for this sort of work. Is it something you would be prepared to try?"

Georgina shuffled from one foot to the other. "Would it hurt?"

"A little but nothing you couldn't handle. Just think of the money! It would probably involve anal as well. You do anal don't you?"

No reply but more blushing and the student dropped her eyes to the floor. "I tried that once and it really hurt," she said in a very small voice.

"Would you do it if it didn't hurt? It only hurts when it's not being done right you know," he lied, thinking of the damage his monster cock would do to the eighteen year old's virgin arsehole.

"Okay then. If the money's good!"

"Let's see what you've got then little Georgie. Come over here."

Sven took his time in fondling the young woman for the camera. He wanted to quickly get her used to being handled before he started reddening her buttocks. His big hands squeezed her tits while she looked away and then slipped down a flat stomach to spread her surprisingly labia open for inspection. "How many men have been inside this pretty pussy Georgina?" He made the question sound matter of fact as he slipped a finger inside her.

"I've had sex with three boyfriends but not at all for a while. Do you mind?" She added as she felt Sven's fingers move inside her.

"If you want to make it in this industry, you need to lose all you inhibitions darling," Sven scolded. He pulled his fingers and at held them in front of the girl's plump lips. "Now clean them and look at the camera."

There was a little hesitation but not much. Georgina had made up her mind. She put out her tongue and began to lick her own juices off Sven's fingers, not resisting when he pushed them into her mouth.

"Very good," Sven told her, finally taking his fingers from Georgina's mouth. "Let's see how well you take a spanking shall we?" He didn't wait for a reply but just pulled his chair out into the middle of the office, where all the cameras were focused on, sat down and pulled the petite young woman down, over his lap.

"I'm not sure…" Georgina was a little disconcerted at the pace of events but Sven was very much in control and didn't intend to ease up at all.

"Stay on your toes and put your hands flat on the floor," Sven ordered and was pleased to see the overawed girl doing exactly as she was told. Her rump was raised nicely in that position and he had a camera positioned just right to capture the plump pussy and wispy red hairs peeking out between slightly parted legs. There was also a camera at the other end and he coaxed her to lift her head and look into the lens as he gently stroked her soft pussy. Despite her waiflike figure, she had a pleasingly round bottom, as though her body had deposited all its fat just on her tits and arse. That made her just perfect for spanking and he told her so. She had potential to make a lot of money if she could learn to take a good spanking he told her.

Once Georgina seemed to have relaxed a little, Sven started the punishment. *Wack!* Her whole body rocked forward under the force of the first blow and a little noise came from deep down in the teenager's throat. Sven paused to check her for damp and sure enough her pussy had already started to gush. That was a good sign.

Once she had taken six whacks, Georgina really started to respond. Her legs began to alternately lift and she began to protest. "Please Sir, that's enough. I've had enough…"

"Tell that to the camera," Sven quipped. "And I'll tell you when you've had enough!" Wh*ack!*

Another five and Georgina's round arse was bright red. She was openly crying and her hips were wiggling from side to side in an involuntary attempt to avoid Sven's hand. "Had enough?"

His question was really academic.

"Yes Sir, please stop. I can't take any more."

That was fine with Sven. The sight of that gorgeous young arse wriggling around was almost too much for him. He had to sink his cock into it and soon. He pulled her to her feet and led her off by the hand. "Time for something different," was all he told the distraught young woman.

A doorway led them into Sven's bedroom. It wasn't wired for video but he knew the only way he was going to get his massive cock into Georgina's tiny anus was on the bed. He wasn't bothered about filming this bit. This was for him. He threw her on to the bed, retrieved a tube of lube from a drawer and climbed up to hold her in place. A finger followed and she protested a little as it slipped in and out to begin loosening her up.

One finger became two and then three. Georgina reached back to grab as his wrists but only held them lightly; not really trying to stop him.

"It's time," Sven announced, slathering his cock in lube and climbing on to the soft backs of Georgina's thighs. His cock instinctively found her hole and the young woman braced herself for what was coming.

Sven started slowly but got nowhere. The pretty student's sphincter was tightly closed and seemed very strong. He gradually increased the pressure and still got nowhere. Finally he was pushing for all his might when suddenly he felt something give and seconds later, he was deep inside Georgina's warm and slippery guts.

The young woman screamed. "Oh fuccccck! Get off me you bastard. Get off!" She bucked for all her might in a vain attempt to dislodge the huge column of gristle that was burning into her but Sven simply looped his arm around her neck and squeezed her throat a little to assert his control.

Once she settled down a little, Sven began to thrust. He was hornier than he could ever remember and this tight little college girl wriggling underneath him was threatening to make his balls explode. He felt her resistance slowly wain and then the tension in her muscles gradually eased off, so he was able to get further and further inside her.

Georgina began to wriggle in a different way and her cries became moans of desire. "Unnnh, yes." She bit her lip and began to push her soft bottom up against him.

Sven was humping into the juicy little female like a battering ram. The slapping noise of flesh against flesh was eclipsed by her cries of passion. His balls were painfully tight and he felt so good, it was amazing. He forced his hands under her soft body and filled his hands with her firm titties, using them as handles to haul her back on to his cock even harder.

It was Georgina who came first. Her body jerked like a dying fish, nailed to the bed by Sven's gigantic cock. "Oh yes! Yes Yeeeees!" Her already tight ring piece clamped around Sven's cock and triggered his impending ejaculation. His arm tightened around her throat so hard as to stop her breathing for a moment as he unloaded a boiling hot load of spunk deep into the helpless girl's bowel.

The aftermath was slightly embarrassing. Sven ushered the girl out of his bedroom before she noticed the lack of cameras. "You did great," he assured her. "I guarantee you're going to be overwhelmed with work as soon as I get your video stitched together. He hedged her questions about how long things would take but assured her he would get back to her as soon as he heard anything.

Georgina slowly pulled on her clothes. She looked exhausted. As she was about to leave, she had a question for Sven. "Can I get my sister an audition?"

"I'm happy to get her details Honey but you know there's no favouritism don't you? What does she look like?"

"We're identical twins."

Sven reigned in his excitement. The possibilities were endless! "Sure, bring her in tomorrow!"

Santa Empties His Sack

*M*arianne turned over and looked at the clock on her bedside table. It was two o'clock in the morning and she was nowhere near feeling sleepy. Her husband was snoring beside her after 'playing Santa' and the kids had exhausted themselves with excitement many hours ago.

A noise downstairs caught her attention and she urgently poked Edward in the back. Christmas Eve was a prime time for burglars and she was not going to let them get away with Kellie and Ed Jnr's new toys. With a disgusted *harrumph* at her lazy husband, she pulled on her fluffy slippers and silk kimono and cautiously made her way down stairs.

"Ho! Ho! Ho! Hi Marianne and Happy Christmas!" The fat, jolly man certainly looked the part and the thirty year old wife and mother found herself smiling, despite herself.

"Very funny! Now who is it? Is that you Steve?" She asked, referring to her joker of a brother.

"Search your heart young lady," Santa told her. "I think you know who I am." He seemed to get closer and Marianne realised that was because she had closed the gap by walking towards him. "Now," he continued. "Do you want to know why I'm here?"

"Hmmm, let me see," the young mother answered sarcastically. "To bring presents to my perfectly behaved children?"

"Ho! Ho! Ho! You wouldn't be talking to me if that was the only reason. I'm in and out in the blink of an eye for that duty. No, I'm here for Santa's Christmas present."

"And what might that be?" Marianne's hands were now

defiantly on her hips.

"Why you of course my dear," Santa roared. "Have a look!"

Marianne looked down at herself and saw to her complete shock that her night clothes had disappeared, to be replaced by a big silk ribbon, wrapped around her body and barely covering her modesty. She was not all ashamed of her sexy body and for good reason but she was well-brought up and quite shy. Her firm breasts pushed against the ribbon and she could see the outline of an erect nipple was very clear. The cool material against her sex indicated that her very obvious labia were also likely to be on display for this jolly fat man. "How, what, who? This is really inappropriate," she stuttered. "…the children…!"

Santa was now stood right inside her personal space and Marianne felt a hard nipple brush against the fur of the front of his coat. "Don't worry about your family, they won't wake," he told her. "Every Christmas Eve my elves select a woman for me," he explained. His gloved hand came up to cup her chin and raised her face towards his. "I have to say, they've chosen rather well." His mouth closed on Marianne's and she subconsciously parted her lips in response.

The naïve housewife's mind was now in turmoil. Fiercely faithful to her one and only love, she had never so much as hugged another man other than her dad and brother and here she was, willingly having her mouth probed by the tongue of a bearded myth. He broke off to let her breathe for a moment and she said the only thing she could think of. "But what about Mrs Christmas…?"

"You don't believe that story do you?" Santa smiled. "This year, you're Mrs. Christmas!" His mouth closed back over Marianne's and his gloved hand found her tits.

Marianne forgot everything except the warm feeling spreading throughout her body. A firm hand on her shoulder pushed her downwards and it seemed the most natural thing in the world to drop to her knees in the family room and unzip Father Christmas. He unfurled in her hand and from that angle looked nothing like the old man he surely must be. His cock hardened under her glare and as it filled with blood; got bigger and bigger.

Glug! Glug! Glug! In no time at all, the naughty housewife was deep throating Santa. Her dainty hand just reached around the base of his sturdy root but the bell end was still reaching well beyond her gullet and into her throat. As she enjoyed his powerful cock on her knees in the shade of her Christmas tree, the *song I saw Mommy kissing Santa Claus* sprang into her mind and she began to giggle around St Nick's meat.

"That was a bit of a slip up on my part," Santa chuckled, as though he could read her mind. "I don't make many mistakes but that was a doozy!" He pulled his housewife to her feet and led her across to the dining table. "Up you pop, my dear," he lifted her by the waist and sat her down on the edge.

The table top was cold against Marianne's bare ass and made her all the more aware of her nakedness. She instinctively lay back on the hard wood and felt her thighs part of their own accord.

Santa's cock was certainly big and it felt enormous as he laid it against her slit. An almost indiscernible movement of his hefty hips lodged the helmet in her porch and then his trouser anaconda began to part her pussy as it wormed its way inside her.

"Ohhh my Goddd!" Marianne began to howl. "You're too big for me, take it out."

Santa chuckled his familiar jolly laugh. "Don't make a fuss little girl," he admonished. "You've popped two babies out of this pretty pussy. I'm sure you can manage my wee man!"

"Your wee man!" Marianne bellowed, the veins popping out on her neck with the exertion. "You're turning me inside out!"

"Ho! Ho! Ho!" Santa Claus was now fully inside his Christmas present and he began to fuck her with a vigor that belied his apparent age.

"Uh! Uh! Uh!" Marianne grunted out loud each time the jolly man dipped inside her. She shook her head and shut her eyes tightly as the pressure built inside her to dangerous levels.

"She really is a prize. Look how her titties jiggle!" A high-pitched voice dragged her back from the depths of her pleasure and for a moment she thought her kids were awake. Her eyes shot open and she found herself staring into deep emerald irises.

The rutting couple was surrounded by about ten odd looking people. About half the size of a human, they had innocent, naive faces but their bodies were anything but. The one who spoke was a female with almost cartoon-like dimensions. She reminded Marianne of Jessica Rabbit, with her exaggerated curves and huge, firm tits.

Santa was now slamming into his mommy-slut but was barely raising a sweat. "Now you've met my elves," he told her. "What do you think of them? They were specially designed by one of my horny forebears!"

Marianne was barely in control of herself by now. Her breath was ragged and her mind was wandering. "You mean you have sex with them?"

"Oh yes!" Santa reached across and tweaked the pretty elfish girl's nipple. "I may only fuck a human woman once a year but my horny elves are always around!"

The idea of the big fat man humping these petite little sexy creatures was enough to push Marianne over the edge. "Oh! Oh! Oh! Yeeees!" Her pussy convulsed around Santa and squeezed his cock.

"That's right my girl," the old man crooned as his hips continued to slam into her. "Get that fertile womb nice and ready for me, 'cos Santa's going to make a baby in you!"

"Oh noooo!" Marianne was barely conscious but that got her attention.

"Oh yeeeees!" Santa's hips gave one last hammer blow and then he stopped dead. His cock pulsed and he emptied a seemingly endless supply of cum inside the helpless housewife.

It took a while for Marianne to get her breath and her wits back but then she leapt on to the attack. "What did you do?" Her tone was accusatory.

Santa lifted his bulk from his latest conquest and zipped himself up. "I told you Marianne," he said matter of factly. "I made a baby in you. Would you like me to explain?"

Marianne said nothing so he continued anyway. "Every few years, my elves pick an extra-special woman for me to inseminate and continue the Santa line. You've been chosen to have one of my sons and in ten months' time, there'll be another little stocking over your fireplace for me to fill."

Marianne was now shocked. "You can't…!"

"Ho! Ho! Ho! Of course I can and I have! When I decide to retire, I will have my pick of heirs to choose from around the world!" Santa held out his hand and helped the well-fucked mommy to her feet. "It's time for a ride in my sleigh now. Are you ready?" Still holding her hand, he walked Marianne towards the fireplace.

In a blink of an eye, the confused young woman found herself high above the rooftops. She was undeniably in Santa's sleigh. Looking over the mountain of presents, she could see the illuminated church steeple of her small town. And despite the snow on the ground and her state of undress, she didn't feel at all cold.

Santa stroked her cheek tenderly. "I've got to go to work now my dear but I have a wild night of entertainment planned for you!" Marianne went to move her arm and realised she couldn't. Looking down, she saw the ribbons had been moved from her body to leave her completely naked and were now wrapped around her wrists and ankles; spreading her wide open and fully displaying her delicious slim body as she lay back against the gift mountain. She saw movement amongst the boxes and realised they were not alone again.

First to speak was the elfish girl. "Can I go first Santa? Pleeeeease?" She begged like a spoilt child.

"Ho! Ho Ho! Of course you can, Kiely. It's your turn" Santa smiled and patted her on the head. "But before you have your fun, why don't you introduce your brothers and sisters."

The little woman giggled, stood upright and let her simple green dress shimmer to the floor. Marianne had never had any sort of attraction for another woman but this creature was just, so... divine! Standing no more than three six, her firm, shapely breasts must have been at least a 34D. Her slim waist led to womanly hips and a cute, shaven pussy. She really was built for sex! She had no doubt she was going to taste her, but first... "Well," tinkled Kiely, "let's see who's first!"

"Me! Me!" The excitable lady-elf was a little less shapely than Kiely but just as luscious.

Kiely's laugh was tick the jingle of bells. "Well, this is my sister Mistletoe" she said. "She's named after her favorite activity; she's the most amazing kisser." With a squeak, Mistletoe crawled over and lowered her juicy lips on Marianne's.

Marianne thought of resisting for just a moment and then she succumbed to the amazing feelings Mistletoe sparked within her. She felt little hands on her naked breasts as the long, pointed tongue thoroughly probed the inside of her mouth and set off tiny electrical sparks against her own tongue.

The Boston housewife was in a daze when the elf finally broke away. "…And this is Tinsel," Kiely continued. "She has rather a way with, erm, tinsel!" This female elf had jet black hair and pointy tits. She wrapped a length of silver tinsel from her waist, held it up for a moment then threw it towards their guest.

Marianne watched in a stupor as the length of shiny wire hovered for a moment and then dropped over her chest, magically wrapping itself around her perfect 34B tits. The girl stepped forward and examined her work with no little satisfaction, patting the housewife's swollen bosoms to emphasise how tender they had suddenly become.

"My next sister is called Holly," Kiely chimed. "See if you can see why!" The new elf had shocking pink hair. She crawled purposely up the woman's body and found a nipple with her mouth.

"Ah!" Marianne cried out in pain and indignation. "You bit me!"

"That'll be it," Kiely laughed. "Now meet some of the boys. This is Nobby!" Marianne's jaw hit her chest as she watched the man-dwarf slowly rubbing his cock as he looked meaningfully at her. His knob was so big it seemed to be half the length of his body.

"And you have to meet Blitz," Kiely continued. "Wanna see why he's called that?" The nimble little man leapt up on to prow of the sleigh and then further still, so he was perched on the rump of a reindeer. He whipped his pecker out and rubbed it furiously for a few seconds. "Here we go!" Kiely laughed and Marianne watched in awe as a glob of cum launched from his cock, arched through the air and hit her straight between the eyes.

"My God!" She cried out. "That must be twenty feet!"

"Mmmm!" Kiely murmured. "Let me help you out with that!" Dropping to her knees, she licked the spunk from the housewife's face and then tasted her lips briefly. Then she patted her cheek and crawled up between her parted thighs.

When the girl's tongue met her pussy lips, Marianne thought she had gone straight to heaven! All her prejudices went straight out of the non-existent window. That single touch, in an instant, reinvented her!

Little Kiely licked Santa's gloopy sperm out of Marianne's box as the sleigh resumed its round the world trip. Looking over the edge as she writhed and moaned under the elfish girl's ministrations, the horny housewife saw familiar landmarks come and go: New York, London, Moscow, Stockholm. They all seemed to pass in the blink of an eye. Kiely wasn't alone, however. A movement in the corner of Marianne's eye revealed Nobby standing at her side with his cock in his hand once more. "Open up sweetheart," he told her and pushed it against her lips.

The obedient housewife opened without so much as a moment's pause of course but as the man elf pushed himself inside the warm cavern of her mouth, she almost regretted doing so. He was just so big, it hurt her jaw to stretch so wide open.

The thick rubbery helmet hit the back of Marianne's mouth and stopped dead just as it made her gag. The elf pushed a couple of times but to no avail; it just bumped up against her glottis; seemingly too big to get any further. The young woman reached up to grab the root of his cock and realised to her absolute astonishment that there was more outside her mouth than in.

At that very moment, Kiely slid her tongue inside her human lover in a long, swiping motion that sent Marianne into orbit. Her back arched and her ass came off the sleigh just as far as her bonds would allow. Her mouth opened even wider around the muscular invader and she emitted a muffled scream.

That was just the reaction the man elf needed. As Marianne opened her throat, he shoved as hard as his little body would allow and completely filled her throat.

She liked to suck cock like the next girl but Marianne found swallowing that sword just a little too much. Her eyes were watering, the drool ran from the corner of her mouth and the snot from her nose. When he eventually withdrew his rock hard tool from her throat she was massively relieved and sucked down big lungsful of air. Her relief soon ran out though when she saw he was headed down her body.

"Christ no!" Marianne cried out as the elf laid the tip of his cock against her pussy mouth. "You're too big; you'll split me in half!"

"Ho! Ho! Ho!" Santa had reappeared on the sleigh. "That's what they all say but Nobby's very talented with that big root of his." The big man selected his next sack of presents before continuing. "My Christmas present last year was a petite eighteen year old virgin who was so tight she could barely get her own finger in her slit. By the end of the night, Nobby and Buddy could get in that cunt together, side by side. She was as slack as an old leather purse by time we'd finished with her."

As Marianne listened to that story with disbelief, Nobby was working his way inside her with tiny movements of his hips. The huge, mushroom-like helmet spread her lips apart like the petals of a flower as he continued his mission. The pressure began to build to an almost intensity when Marianne's attention was distracted again by two pairs of soft lips, clamping down on her erect nipples. Her pussy burned a little as the big cock burrowed inside her and she was fascinated by the sight of the little man crouched over her groin as he plumbed her depths. And then her field of view was blocked as Kiely swung her leg over the helpless woman's head and Marianne tasted pussy for the first time.

Time seemed to pass in slow motion as Marianne was used by the elves. Male or female, they all had a go at her. She sucked cock and ate pussy. An elf called Glitter sprinkled some sort of fairy dust on her body and had the woman taste her – Marianne thought she tasted like marzipan and mulled wine. Jingle had the biggest balls imaginable, hanging low and heavy. As he humped her they banged against her pussy and inner thighs, while his brothers and sisters sang *Jingle balls. Jingle all the way....* An annoying little elf-man called Nick then squished mince pies thoroughly into her body and the little people feasted on it; immersing the frustrated woman in a tongue bath. Then Marianne was rolled on to her hands and knees to be spit roasted by two huge cocks. It seemed to the tired housewife that days had passed when the elves had finally had their fill, leaving her to collapse on the soft floor of the sleigh with cum running from her every hole.

"Ho! Ho! Ho!" Santa roared. "That's another Christmas delivery finished. Now where's my present gone?" He spied the exhausted woman on the floor and patted his knee. "Come up on to my lap little girl and tell me what you'd like for Christmas."

Despite herself, Marianne got straight up and walked obediently over to the big man, stepping around him to sit on his thigh. "Not like that," Santa roared with mirth and grabbed her arm to spin her around. Confused for just a minute as she was manhandled, her destination was soon apparent. Santa bent her over his knee.

"Wha, what are you doing, Santa?" Marianne stuttered, as though his intention were not completely obvious.

"Well, young lady," he chuckled as he stroked her downy butt cheeks. "I have the knack of telling whether someone has been naughty or nice and I've decided you have been naughty" A fat finger slipped inside her slippery cunt, as though by accident.

"Don't I get a lump of coal then?" Marianne pleaded.

"Don't believe everything you read about me!" Santa's gloved hand descended on the mommy's firm buttock. "I have far more effective corrections for bad behavior!"

"Ahh! Ahh! Ahh!" Marianne's wistful cries carried far and wide through the crisp winter night. She hadn't been spanked by anyone since the age of eight and was finding it an educational experience to say the least. He ass cheeks burned like crazy and it was an odd sort of pain that spread a strange warmth through her whole lower body. Santa's unyielding hand showered a fusillade of blows on her unpadded rear and she soon began to dance around his lap, lost to a mixture of pain and pleasure.

"Ohhh no, please Santa, I'll be good. Reeeeally good!" The tears had begun to run down the sexy woman's cheeks but it wasn't pain that was now driving her mad.

Eventually the punishment finished. "Let's see how good you can be Marianne," Santa chuckled. "Come and sit on my lap."

Marianne picked herself up and turned sideways to slide her fanny on to the big man's thigh. Santa caught her by the waist and effortlessly spun her around. "Not like that little girl," he roared. "Pop up here!"

Up here was a reference to a very erect cock that was sticking out of Santa's red pants in a very obvious invitation. Now straddling his thighs, a boost from his white-gloved hands that were still around her waist was enough to pop her sloppy pussy on to the angry looking root. As she slid down, Marianne let go a mournful moan, "uhhhhhhhhhh!"

Santa's sleigh zipped over the Statue of Liberty at the exact moment that Marianne came all over his big, red cock. The poor girl was exhausted by now and was as limp as a rag doll as he picked her up again and spread her on her front. "Now for your Christmas present, Mrs. Limber," he bellowed.

And Marianne's Christmas present was to be buggered by Father Christmas. An elven tongue slobbered around her smallest hole as she passively lay still and waited for him to take her. He shifted his significant bulk around and she felt the weight of him on the rear of her thighs. His cockhead touched her anus lightly and made her jump and then the pressure began to build.

"I haven't... I can't...!" Marianne began to weakly protest her anal virginity but of course it had no effect. Santa was on a mission. He loved to break in a housewife's back doors and he'd been promising himself this treat for the whole of that long Christmas night.

"Oh God, no! Marianne began to struggle as the fat cock started to worm its way inside her tight, tight rear passage. As Santa rubbed his big knob around her anus, Marianne wriggled from side to side in a half-hearted attempt to stop him getting in. Slowly but surely, he began to push his massive cock against her tiny little opening. Gradually her sphincter began to give under the pressure and bit by bit, he edged inside her.

Marianne had now become very animated and shook her head from side to side, her cries for help, drifted on the crisp night air for a few moments until Kiely slid back under her face again and the sound was lost inside the elf's sodden fuck tunnel. Her ass squirmed desperately in every direction but there was no escape from the onslaught. Suddenly with a big thrust, Santa buried himself fully inside the milf's luscious booty. Simultaneously her head whipped back and Marianne let out a loud, strangled moan of pain and pleasure before flopping back forward again to continue servicing her new girlfriend. Now inside, Santa wasted no time in humping her ass, thrusting hard and fast until he finally emptied his sack deep inside her guts.

Without ceremony, the big man pulled out of Marianne's snug little anus. Standing up straight, he reached into a pocket and produced something small and black. Pushing the plug into her leaky ass, he slapped her butt cheek hard and laughed out loud. "That will keep my little present safe until Christmas morning! Ho!

Ho! Ho!" Marianne fell into a deep sleep with Santa's deep and jolly laugh echoing in her ears.

"Happy Christmas Mommy! Come on, let's see if Santa came!" Marianne woke with a groan to the sound of excited kids. She had had the weirdest of dreams. Turning on to her side and; reaching for her robe, she felt stiff as hell, as though she had done ten rounds with Mike Tyson.

As she rolled over on to her fanny, she stopped dead. Checking that no one was looking at her, she surreptitiously reached behind her and felt her butt hole with her fingertips. Sticking a good three inches out of her ass was a thick rubber plug! *Shit! Where the hell could she get a home pregnancy test on Christmas morning?*

The Governor's Wife

Steve couldn't help himself. There were a few desirable women at the Governor's reception but the most desirable was, as always, the most unavailable. When the Governor shook his hand on the way in, his eyes were on his wife; Tamara. His probing stare always left a woman uncomfortable but at that stage they never knew why. Tamara would soon find out. Once he crossed eyes with the geeky, well bred forty something Governor's wife, he knew instantly something about Tamara that she didn't know herself. Tamara was very submissive.

The thing was though, for Steve, there was no such thing as an unavailable woman. He never really knew what had happened to him on the alien spaceship when he had been abducted but when he woke up on an Arizona desert road three weeks later, Steve was a different man. He had acquired several, well, superhuman abilities. Above all else though, he had the ability to control other people and persuade them to do his bidding. It worked with men okay but was far more effective with women. And the more submissive the woman's nature, the more effective the control. Following that experience, it took Steve several years to come to terms with what he now was. He tried to settle back down in his previous life of plumbing, drinking and being rejected by women but he couldn't. He met a different woman every night. He fucked her, knocked her up and moved on, with the hapless girl left with a swelling belly and no idea he was the father. That was all very well but no matter how big and apparently anonymous his community seemed to be, people started to notice things. Once the questions started, he packed and left. Steve drifted for a few years, trying to find himself and eventually ended up in Bermuda; a small British outpost in the middle of nowhere.

It took her the best part of an hour to find the time but inevitably Tamara wandered across to the group he was engaging with his wit and humour. "Tamara!" She introduced herself with a traditional stiff English handshake.

"Hello Tamara!" He excused himself from the group to focus his attention on her. "I was wondering how long it would take you to come over."

"Yes, well, official guests…" His gaze stopped her mid-bluster. "What do you do?"

"I'm Steve," he smiled. "And don't get so hung up on what people do. It's who we are that's more important."

"Yes, yes, of course." Tamara was floundering, unable to understand why she was on the back foot for possibly the first time in her adult life. She was always the one in control.

Steve fixed her with a steady gaze and subtly held her arm as her balance went a little. "I understand your husband leaves for a week in the UK tomorrow, Tamara?"

"Errm, yes, he does."

"Good. Then I'd like to dine with you. I'll be back here at seven pm tomorrow." He released her arm and added, "It'll give me a chance to get to know you better." He touched her arm again before moving away. "A lot better," he whispered. He then turned his back to her to chat to a twenty something blonde with big tits and bleached teeth; leaving Tamara seething and curiously jealous.

The next morning was a confusing time for Tamara. She kissed her husband goodbye first thing and busied herself around the house. She knew she was inviting a strange man into the Residence for dinner but she was damned if she could remember why. For some reason, the naïve socialite thought it was best to give the chef the night off and cook herself, which she rarely did. She then spent much of the rest of the day tidying things and then beautifying herself. She was alone in the huge house once the Governor had left. Her eighteen year old daughter was due back from her UK university on the next flight in two days but until then it was just her and the staff; who were themselves only part-timers.

It took her several hours to come up with the right recipe

but eventually Tamara decided on coq au vin because it was easy but a little upper-class. Like herself, she thought to herself for a split second and then admonished herself for the idea. Where the hell did that come from? She shook it off and continued shaving her legs.

Seven o'clock came around in no time but there was no knock at the door. Tamara immediately began to feel anxious that Steve might not show, although she still had no idea why she had invited him round. She poured herself another sherry and checked her pixie-cut auburn hair in the hall mirror.

It was a full twenty-five minutes past the hour when Steve finally rang the bell. There was no real reason for his lateness, he had simply learned that his women were even more malleable if he kept them on edge. He had a bottle of champagne in his hand and knew how to use that to his advantage too. "Hello Tamara," he greeted her. "You look good enough to eat tonight." He looked her up and down meaningfully, undressing her with his eyes, before stepping forward, grabbing her by the waist and pulling her towards him to kiss the surprised wife on the lips. "But let's eat whatever that delicacy is that I can smell first." He released her and patted her bottom on the way past.

Tamara was speechless and confused. She showed him through to the family lounge and offered champagne flutes when he popped the cork. "Here's to a pleasurable evening," he toasted, his eyes never leaving Tamara.

The meal was all pretty normal. Tamara consumed several glasses of claret with the delicious dish and soon felt light-headed. The conversation was also normal... for a time. Tamara rabbited on about her life as the first lady of Bermuda and what her family was up to. Steve had only questions; telling her very little about himself as was his wont. He never took his eyes of her though and as the meal progressed, the susceptible woman fell further and further under his powerful spell. When their plates were finally empty and Tamara offered cheesecake or a cheeseboard, Steve changed the agenda. "Why am I here Tamara?" He propped his elbows on the table and rested his chin on his fists as he gazed at her.

"I don't really know Steve. Why are you here?" Tamara looked back at him with wide eyes like a bush baby. "You said you wanted to get to know me," Tamara was suddenly very nervous again. "What do you want to know?"

Steve chuckled softly. "Oh Tamara, the knowledge I want of you can't be discovered with words." He stood and walked the length of the dining table; Tamara's eyes following him until he disappeared behind her. He rested his hands on the hostess's delicate shoulders. "What I need to know about you Tamara," he whispered in her ear, "is how you look naked, how your charming breasts feel in my hands, how your juices taste on my tongue, how cute your face looks when I ram my cock into you and how delicious you feel when wrapped around my tool." He slid his hands down her shoulders and found the zip of her dress, opening it all the way.

"I can't," Tamara whimpered. "My husband…"

"But you will," Steve answered as his hands now found her firm breasts; slipping into her silky bra. "You will because you can't help yourself. You are so horny and need me more than anything else in the world, don't you?"

Tamara's murmur was so low that Steve hardly heard the inevitable reply. "Yes!"

Steve took Tamara by the hand and drew her to her feet, pushing her evening dress down her arms for it to fall around her feet, leaving her stood only in her matching bra and panties, jewellery and heels. "Good enough to eat indeed," he chuckled, pulled her into him and his mouth found hers, slipping his tongue into her mouth and snogged her passionately as his hand played along her body. His nimble fingers found her bra catch and deftly unclipped it, pushing the straps down her slim shoulders and letting the cups drop into his hands. He tweaked the painfully erect nipples between his finger and thumb and the helpless wife bit her lip as Steve sucked each of her nubs into his mouth in turn.

Steve took his time in pleasuring Tamara with his mouth and his fingers. He sucked her teats hard as though trying to draw milk from them and his fingers found her anxious pussy mouth to warm that up for his pleasure. When Steve finally stepped back to appraise the Governor's wife in all her naked glory, she was a quivering wreck. Her plump, rouged lips were parted slightly as she panted in passion; her little round boobs rising and falling at the same time. He ran an appreciative hand down her toned torso and enjoyed the feeling of her warm and vibrant skin. She was a natural beauty but nonetheless as fit as gym bunnies ten years younger. He cupped her smooth cheek in one hand. "Do you suck your husband's cock?"

Tamara recoiled from his words; shocked in a way that his hands hadn't bothered her. She just wasn't used to such coarse language. "Not as a rule," she answered.

Steve smiled. "You'll suck mine though won't you?" It wasn't really a question. He knew the answer.

"Of course I will!"

"Tell me in your posh accent that you would like to suck my cock."

"I would like to suck your cock, Steve."

Hearing such a suggestion from Tamara in her cut glass, aristocratic voice made Steve rock hard all of a sudden. His hand dropped to her shoulder and gently pushed her to her knees. "Show me what you've got my lover!"

His lover! Is that what she was all of a sudden? How did that happen? It felt good though. Tamara unzipped his fly and reached inside, enjoying the feel of his rampant maleness. As she drew his penis out into view, she blinked at the size of him. Maybe she just wasn't used to seeing them like this anymore, or, maybe...! There was no denying it. He was huge! She rubbed a hand up and down the muscular shaft a view times and the feeling of power in her hand astounded her. The repressed posh girl had never in all her forty four years experienced anything like this.

The rampant member bumped against her pursed lips. "Open your mouth and pop it in," Steve urged and Tamara did exactly that. She felt a little discomfort as her lips stretched to accommodate his girth and then his rubbery helmet was bumping along the ridges on the roof of her mouth. Then she gagged!

Steve laughed as the posh wife pushed him away and looked, just for a moment, to be about to throw up. "Don't be so keen to deep throat me, you horny little slut! We'll get there soon so take your time."

Horny little slut? Her? The situation was getting so surreal, Tamara almost felt she was detached from it. Sort of looking in at some dirty girl who looked like her, doing things she would never dream of. She opened her mouth again and began to suck gently on the tip of Steve's big babymaker as she firmly wanked him again.

It was a gradual process this time but Steve gradually worked his way into the posh wife's mouth until he was once again prodding at her glottis. And this time he didn't stop. Holding Tamara's small head firmly in both hands, he built the pressure until he popped into her throat. Her petite hands rested on his upper thighs, as though ready for resistance but not daring or wanting to exploit it. He pushed a bit further and saw the panic register in her eyes and her fists ball; although they didn't push against him. "Hands behind your back," he commanded gently and she immediately obeyed. Then he began his rhythm of fucking her pretty proud face with his fat cock.

As he relished the feeling of Tamara's soft mouth on his rampant cock, Steve looked up to see the face of an angel. A portrait photo across the room was of a much younger version of the Governor's wife, but with blonde hair and wider eyes; the latter feature giving the girl a desirable innocence that made his balls ache. Tucking that image away until later, he took a firmer hold of the lady's head and began to skull fuck her hard.

Steve loved a good blowjob and far better when it was a woman unused to so serving a man. He was after all a great trainer. Her soft mouth enveloped his tender shaft and she had the instinctive common sense to keep her teeth well away from him. Apart from the great sensations of a woman's mouth, lips, tongue and throat on his glans, it was also good symbolism. Having a proud, independent woman on her knees in front of him as he used her face for his pleasure was excellent training for any submissive and a real buzz for him. Her blue eyes looked up at him as he rammed his cock in and out and transmitted unbridled subservience.

The steady stimulation of his cock had only one inevitable conclusion and when Steve came it was a volcanic eruption. He didn't bother to warn her; that was part of the fun. There was no doubt Tamara had yet to experience the honour of swallowing a man's cum and Steve was a pretty advanced subject for her first. Her only warning of the oncoming storm, if she was astute enough to observe it, was a slight tightening of his hands on her head and an upping of the pace he was smashing his cock down her throat. Then he suddenly stiffened and his sour tasting cream filled her throat.

She swallowed the first glob. That was a reflex action.
Then his balls kept on pumping. Her mouth filled and she tried to
pull away as it overflowed along his shaft and then out of her nose.
When he finally released her to fall in a retching heap on the floor,
Tamara's face was a mess of jism, saliva, snot and mascara. At that
moment, she was no longer the proud Governor's wife. Tamara
was Steve's slut. No more and no less.

The adventure was far from over though. Steve was fully
capable of going again straight away. That was another gift from
his time with the aliens. He wanted to play a bit before fucking her
though. "Bend over the table," he told her.

Tamara cleaned her face with a napkin and did exactly as
she was told as always. She rested her bosoms and her folded arms
on the hard table top; her head cradled on her forearms. Pushing
her bottom back and arching her back, she presented Steve with a
perfectly heart-shaped arse.

Steve sat on the floor between her spread legs and took his
time in studying the posh totty's twat. He laid his big hands on her
soft buttocks and felt her quiver under his touch. Spreading her
labia open with his thumbs, he looked past the light ginger fuzz,
straight into Tamara's body. Her cunt was already quivering open
and ready for cock. She would be literally gagging for it soon.

His first taste of the Governor's wife was one Steve would
remember for a long time. Every pussy he had eaten tasted
different and this lady certainly had a sweet one. He licked along
the lips and then slid his long tongue straight inside her; holding
her up as she shuddered and almost fell.

Tamara had never experienced cunnilingus. Not like that
anyway. Her husband had once put his head down there and given
her a few exploratory licks but soon got tired of it. This man was
an aficionado. Every touch and movement seemed designed to
inflict upon her the maximum amount of pleasure.

She came in his mouth in a long, shuddering orgasm and
immediately felt ashamed of herself for some reason. Steve stood
and pulled the belt off his trousers. He had raised her pleasure
threshold and now he wanted to teach her the pleasure in pain. He
placed a strong hand in the small of her back and pushed her firmly
down on to the table top. "You will learn a little humility now," he

told her. "Embrace the pain and take your pleasure." He swung his arm and Tamara screamed.

The next few minutes were the most intense imaginable for the Governor's wife. Tamara had never been as much as spanked throughout her spoilt life; not even as a child. Each lash of the belt make her jolt and yelp and her rear quarters got steadily hotter and damper. Finally Steve judged she could not be any more ready and he could no longer resist the temptation to sink his cock into her. He eased her firm buttocks apart with his fingers. "Do you want my cock now Mrs Chamberlain?"

She had no other answer but yes. Despite her brain still saying clearly no because it could see no reason to say yes, every cell of her body was screaming out to be taken by this man. She felt the bruising head of his penis nestle in her gaping pussy mouth and it was as though an electrical circuit was completing between them. "Please," she moaned.

"Please what?"

"Please take me!"

"Do you mean fuck you?" Steve was now making little circles just inside her that were driving Tamara mad.

"Please fuck me," Tamara said automatically; using that word for possibly the first time in her sheltered life.

Steve obliged. He pushed his hefty cock straight into the petite woman and she howled out loud. "Uhhhhh! Oh my goodness! That's, so... Good!"

It was a savage fucking because that was how Steve liked to take a woman. For Tamara though. This was an experience so alien to her that she was losing her grip of reality. His hands moved from her slim hips, to her engorged clitoris, to her sensitive tits, as he hammered his essence into her.

Steve was of course going to breed her. He always did. But he wanted to see her face at the moment his seed fed her uterus. He pulled out to a disappointed grunt from the ruined wife. In one movement he then turned her around and lifted her up, to seat her on the table. Pulling her hips forward and pushing her shoulders down to the woods and then he was inside her again.

Tamara's face was indeed a picture. Steve's cock was big by any standards and was covered with thick, roping veins. Every time one of those lumps and bumps rubbed against her sensitive flesh, it sent a frisson of pleasure through Tamara that was advertised all over her face. He leant over and squeezed her lovely little tits in his hands; nibbling on her upper lip as he relentlessly pounded her pussy.

He didn't warn her he was going to cum. She was so lost in his enchantment that she hadn't considered the effect of his virile sperm hitting her unprotected womb. If she had known his seed was genetically improved to guarantee a hundred percent hit rate, Tamara may have been all the more concerned. As it was, the first indication of her breeding was Steve stiffening a split second before sending waves of hot spunk to splatter all over her insides.

"You weren't wearing a condom," the Governor's wife said matter of factly when she got her breath back.

"That's right," Steve grinned. "Better fuck your husband as soon as he gets back cos you're having my baby."

Tamara lay back and thought about that for a moment. It gave her an odd, warm feeling. She had given up on the idea of another baby many years ago but the idea of this strange man's child growing inside her excited her beyond belief. It excited her almost as much as the impregnation had. And that was a lot!

"Hey," Steve said as he pulled his now flaccid meat from the wife's sloppy cunt with an audible pop. "Who's the horny little blonde in the picture?"

"Oh, that's Anastasia; my daughter."

"How old?"

"She's eighteen on Saturday. She's reading law at Cambridge and gets back for a holiday on Friday."

"Perfect! I want her," Steve told her almost conversationally. "She can join us for dinner on Sunday."

"Okay," agreed Tamara, as though a request to offer up her only daughter for ravishing was the most normal thing in the world.

"I'll see you then," Steve kissed her chastely, as her husband might and left the Governor's wife in the pool of cum that was pooling in the middle of the Residency's dining table.

The Nursing Mother

Sharon was tired and irritable. The truth of the matter was the extra hours she was putting in at the nursing home were making her late for Joel's feeds and the milk just wasn't going anywhere. On top of that, her money problems had reached a head and there was no way she could see that she was going to be able to find the month's rent. Trying to put all that behind her, she adjusted the nursing bra around her rock hard boobs and went to get Mr Cunningham comfortable.

Actually, Mr Cunningham was her favourite resident and that made things much better. The eighty three year old widower was a very charming man and still handsome. He used to be a wealthy farmer he had told her. The owner of the biggest Jersey dairy herd outside the island of the same name. Two years before, his wife had died unexpectedly and it hit him hard. Seeming to give up on life, he aged rapidly and his children found the well-appointed nursing home to be the best solution.

Mr Cunningham's body may have become decrepit but his mind was as agile as ever and so was his libido. Leaning over her client to tuck him in was enough to give him a very obvious erection and he rarely kept his hands to himself. Like most of the elderly men at the home and some of the women, he considered Sharon's voluptuous body to be available for fondling whenever it came into range. Sharon tolerated it and to be honest, quite enjoyed the attention. There was no man in the single mother's life and hadn't been for some time so the brief thrill she got from those gnarled hands set up her nightly masturbatory sessions.

Once she had him settled down for the night, Sharon always found time to chat to the interesting old man for a few minutes.

Usually they talked about his farming business and the places he had travelled to but this time the conversation was all about her. She just couldn't help herself unloading all her difficulties to one of her only friends and in no time he knew all about her money situation.

"But that is not your only problem is it?" Mr Cunningham's voice was still rich and melodic. Sharon found it quite soothing.

"What do you mean Mr Cunningham?" Sharon shifted her position to ease the pressure on her bloated breasts.

He chuckled. "That's exactly what I mean. "You know what sort of farm I ran with my wife don't you?"

"A dairy farm."

"Yes a dairy farm. But it wasn't just cows we used to milk!"

Sharon was now hooked. She leaned over the bed and pretended to ignore the hand that closed gently over her breast. "So what else did you used to milk Mr Cunningham?"

"We used to milk young women and my son still does!" he smiled at the shocked look on Sharon's face as she sat back upright, wresting her tit from his hand.

"There's a very lucrative market out there for woman's milk," the old man went on. "And there's no shortage of young women with surplus milk and not enough money."

"Yeah, that's for sure!" Sharon couldn't help but agree.

"So what about it?" Mr Cunningham grinned like a schoolboy.

"What about what," Sharon replied slowly, the penny only dropping slowly.

"How much is your rent?

"Six hundred and fifty pounds. Why?"

The old man sat up in bed, re-energised. "It's simple, my dear. You get your pretty little arse over here and let me suck the milk from your teats and I will cover your rent this month. What do you say?"

Sharon was shocked. She stood up was just rooted to the spot for a few moments, speechless, before eventually finding a voice. "You're not serious, surely? I mean, that's just so… inappropriate!"

Cunningham reached into his bedside cabinet and drew out a wallet stuffed with fifties. "I'm always serious when it comes to business," he grinned, dropping a handful on to the bed. "Don't think about it anymore. Just lock the door and come here."

When Sharon looked back at her life and considered how it had taken such a direction, she recognised this as the pivotal moment. The twenty six year old redhead never knew why she made the decision she had but without much thought at all she locked the door and walked back to the bed.

"It will work best if you straddle my legs. I mean sit on my lap," Cunningham told her and took her hand as she climbed on to the bed and sat on the duvet, over a predictably hard erection. "You'll need to undo the buttons," he added. "My fingers don't work so well any more."

Slowly unbuttoning her blouse, Sharon watched the old man's face as she did so. He was clearly very excited and seemed at last to have a purpose once again. Maybe that was what had made her mind up. The transaction did not just offer an opportunity both to relieve the stress on her bank account and her bra but also the chance to make this dear old man happy again. How could she have refused?

When she worked the front clasp and her fat tits fell free, Sharon was sure the old man started dribbling. She had just a moment to think about that though as he reached behind her back to draw her closer and his mouth closed on her engorged nipple.

Sharon was very used to feeding her baby and had of course had the odd man play with her tits as a rushed bit of foreplay, this was something entirely different though. The man sucked her far harder than she had ever experienced and it almost hurt. The sensation was quite erotic though, sending a signal straight down to her pussy and making her just ache for orgasm.

The feeding went on until her left breast was completely dry and then he moved on to the right. Throughout the whole session, Sharon was writhing, moaning, crying; just desperate to cum.

Finally, he emptied her and Sharon collapsed on to the bed; helpless and almost whimpering as he continued to fondle her. "Did you enjoy that?" His question when it came was almost silly; it was so obvious she had.

"Oh yes," she moaned. "It was just amazing!"

"Well, your money is underneath you," Cunningham chuckled. "But if you could possibly do something else for me, I will happily double it!"

Sharon rolled on to her front. "And what might that be," she asked, although it was very obviously poking her in the eye.

"Well," Cunningham seemed almost sheepish. "It seems I need milking too! If you could perhaps return the favour with your mouth..?"

Sharon ripped the duvet off the old man and smiled at his seven inch cock, rock hard and already in his hand. "I think I owe you a bit more than that," she whispered as she reached under her skirt and urgently peeled down her knickers.

Sharon was so ridiculously wet, she sank straight down on the old man's cock, barely feeling it enter her. Cunningham reached up to squeeze her still sensitive tits as she bounced up and down. Each time his long prick connected with her cervix, she let out a high-pitched little dry that heightened his excitement.

If the horny young woman thought this was going to be a quickie, she could not have been more mistaken, she could not have been more wrong. Mr Cunningham was as hard as a teenager but had far more staying power. Reaching up to grip the yummy mummy by the hips, he buried his face in her tits and began to hump upwards.

Sharon had no idea how long she spent on that amazing cock. He humped her through first one orgasm and then another. If she had scarcely felt him enter, that was no longer the case. Each upwards movement of the old man's hips pushed his fat shaft further into her, pushing against her pussy walls and banging up against the entrance to her womb.

Her third orgasm was just mind blowing. She collapsed on top of the old man and was vaguely aware of his warm cum sploshing inside her. As she rode the roller coaster of pleasure, she wondered dreamily if he was still capable of getting her pregnant.

As Sharon finally came down to reality, she became aware of a real fuss at the door. People were banging and shouting and it was clear their antics had not been as private as she had intended. Cunningham reached into his wallet and passed her a business card. "I think I may have cost you your job," he told her sheepishly. "Go and see my son and his wife. They will look after you well." Sharon climbed off the bed and kissed him on the forehead as she rearranged her clothes and picked up all the cash off the bed, as well as another big wad he handed over. She opened the door and kept walking.

By the time she had got home, there was already an answerphone message from the night manager and it made her position very clear. "Do not report for work tomorrow evening. You have a disciplinary interview at ten o'clock on Wednesday." As she warmed a bottle for Joel, she turned the business card in her hand. It was very professionally produced and had two names on it, Aaron and Siobhan Cunningham, with an address, email and phone number. While she waited for the milk to warm out, she pulled out her laptop and sent a quick email.

Two days later, Sharon was pulling into a farmyard with Joel asleep in his baby seat in the back. It looked just like any normal farm but the young woman knew better. No one came to meet her so she made her way into the office building near the gate, baby in hand. Finally she came to a door with Siobhan's name on the door. She knocked firmly and when a female voice called out she pushed the door open and entered.

Sharon was unsure what to expect but Siobhan's appearance took her aback. She looked younger than herself, surely no older than early twenties and she was absolutely gorgeous. A platinum blonde, she was tall, shapely and had a friendly smile than instantly put the single mum at ease. "Welcome to Cunninghams," she gushed, standing and holding out her hand. "The biggest dairy farm in South West England."

Before Sharon had time to answer, baby Joel made his presence known with a lung-busting cry.

"Ahh, he's hungry," Siobhan laughed; a delightful tinkling sound like sleigh bells. "Sit down and feed him while we wait for my husband. I love babies." Sharon hesitated for a moment and then Joel roared again and made her mind up for her. She sat down in a huge armchair next to the desk, unbuttoned her blouse and unclipped her nursing bra, holding her big boob up for baby to latch on.

If Sharon thought the boss lady was going to leave her in private to feed her baby, she was very mistaken. Siobhan just sat back in her office chair and watched avidly as Joel suckled on his mother's teat. Her expression was more than a little disconcerting; her eyes seemed full of lust and the end of her tongue ran slowly back and forth along her lips as though she was imaging licking the other woman's milk from them.

Joel sucked one tit dry and Sharon winded him, before heaving him across to the other. Siobhan's eyes never left the naked and now empty boob and Sharon now felt very self-conscious.

That insecurity doubled a moment later when the door crashed open and a man burst in. Sharon subconsciously covered her nude breast and held her baby tighter.

The man was quite clearly Siobhan's husband, although he looked twice her age. He was fit though and as he bent to kiss her cheek, she felt a tingle in her lady parts. His first words to her were succinct and to the point. "You're in!"

"Just like that darling?" Siobhan purred. "Don't you even want to taste her milk?"

"Of course," he smiled. "But if it's good enough for the wee fellah. It's good enough for me." The cute baby was now sitting back on his mother's lap, gurgling with milk running down the side of his mouth. "Come," he took Sharon's hand. "Let us show you around."

"Starting with the nursery," his wife added.

"I'm Aaron Cunningham by the way," the middle-aged man finally introduced himself. "I believe you've met my father?"

"You look a lot alike. Is that where the similarity ends?"

"You'll soon see," Aaron told her cryptically.

The nursery was very impressive and full of babies and toddlers. There were three young women in there, all blondes like herself, who were looking after the children. Two were changing nappies and the third was feeding a baby with a shock of black hair on her breast.

"Let me introduce you to Penny, Sally and Susan," Aaron told her.

"Hiya," the three called out together like bimbos.

"Hello," Sharon replied, rather stiffly.

"Our girls take it in turns to run the nursery. You'll have a stint too," Aaron told her. "The rest of the time, you'll be busy, erm earning your money."

"Oh!" Sharon had assumed they were actual nannies and wondered were Aaron and Siobhan had managed to get three such brainless young women from. All the same, she allowed Penny to take her baby and settle him down to sleep in one of the cots as her hosts led her onwards.

The next room was a real shock. It was massive and filled with a curious sight. There was station upon station with a bench thing and machinery. Lots of tubes and pipes and tanks filled the room and at the far end, Sharon could just see that several of the stations were occupied. "This is where it all happens," Aaron told her. "Welcome to the milking shed."

As they got further, Sharon saw the women were completely naked. Two of them were brunettes and one a redhead like herself. They were bent forward on to the padded benches; their swollen breasts hanging freely beneath them were enclosed in big rubberised cups with plastic tubes sprouting from them. As she got closer, she noticed two other things. They were all secured onto the benches with straps around their waists and wrists and they were producing huge amounts of milk; the transparent tubes were pumping pints of milk into the tanks.

"We give all of the girls a milk accelerant," Aaron explained. "It's perfectly harmless and makes you all huge producers."

"Will I need to have this drug?" Sharon was looking suspiciously at the attendants with the three women. Each of them had a young man behind them and each was casually stroking his charge's loins and buttocks in an apparently caring and asexual way as the women writhed in response to their milking. That struck Sharon as odd and she couldn't help wondering if they were waiting for her to leave before fucking the girls and also whether it would be consensual. The women certainly didn't seem to mind the contact; lost in a world of orgasmic milking as they were.

"If you want to work for us then the jab is a requirement," Aaron answered matter-of-factly. "You'll have your first jab in a few minutes when my wife does your medical."

"Your wife?"

It was Siobhan you answered. "I'm the farm vet," she joked. "Don't worry. A little prick or two for four hundred pounds a week tax free with free board and lodging is a great deal, trust me!"

It was the first time anyone had mentioned the money and Sharon's ears pricked up. All of a sudden the idea of being one of this naked women on display while being milked like a heifer was bearable. That amount of money sitting in her bank account would get her back on her feet in no time. "Where do I sign," she joked back.

"No need to sign," Siobhan told her, steering her out of the big room by her elbow. "Let's get your check-up out the way."

Siobhan at last donned a white coat and Aaron left them be but Sharon still felt very self-conscious standing in front of this woman who seemed to be undressing her with her eyes every time she looked at her. "I need you completely naked," Siobhan told her and seemed to confirm her suspicions.

"Completely?" Sharon asked. "Is there anywhere to change?"

Siobhan's eyes seemed to be laughing at her but the rest of her face didn't change. "Right there will do," she indicated the floor in the middle of the examination room. "There's only us girls, there's no need to be shy!"

Seeing no real alternative, Sharon slowly unbuttoned her blouse and slipped it off her shoulders to place it carefully on the back of a chair, followed by her skirt. She wore no tights as the weather was so warm and so stood just in bra, panties and shoes. "The bra too," Siobhan told her. "You can leave the shoes on and I'll take your knickers off when I have a look down there!" Sharon's face reddened at the idea. The way she worded it didn't make it sound like a regular gynae inspection.

The medical started in a fairly normal way with Siobhan looking in her eyes, mouth and ears. Then she tested her glands and listened to her chest, before a breast exam. "Hmm, they really are a great pair," Siobhan told her somewhat unprofessionally as she weighed the two sizeable top bollocks in her hands. Sharon thought of protesting for a moment but couldn't find the words.

The moment passed quickly as the gorgeous doctor stopped pawing her for a moment. "Hop up on the table then," she ordered. "It's time for a look inside!" She helped her up on to her back and then hooked her fingers into the girl's delicate underwear. "Lift your hips," she coaxed. Sharon did so and Siobhan peeled the panties down her slender legs and off. Sharon's face immediately flushed brighter than her hair. This single act oddly embarrassed her more than anything else that had happened so far that day.

Siobhan didn't bother with gloves but she did use lots of lubricant, much to Sharon's relief. She probed around Sharon's pussy with two fingers for a couple of minutes and the vulnerable young woman had to bite her lip each time a finger bumped against her clitoris, it just felt so good. Seemingly absorbed in this task, Siobhan was silent for a few minutes as she explored the other girl's sex. When she finally spoke, it was inappropriate once again. "I find it hard to believe you've pushed a baby out of here. You're as tight as a virgin!"

"I can assure you I have…!" a finger touched her clit again and Sharon caught her breath before continuing. "You've seen the evidence."

"Indeed!" Siobhan was grinning like a Cheshire cat. "You're certainly healthy enough for the programme." She whipped her fingers out and was pleased to hear a little groan. "Stay in the stirrups," she commanded as she readied a hypodermic syringe, prepared a tiny vein on the underside of Sharon's nipple. "Be brave, this is going to sting a little."

She wasn't joking either. It really hurt! Sharon lay back and closed her eyes as the nipple throbbed, waiting for it to subside.

But it didn't. The throbbing grew and then spread to the other breast. It just felt like her tits were getting bigger and bigger and ready to explode. She squirmed around on the doctor's couch and began to moan in discomfort and frustration.

"Sssh! It will soon pass," Siobhan soothed her. He hands moved to the young woman's bosoms and she began to massage them. Sharon's moaning didn't stop but it changed. She really appreciated the feeling of those hands upon her. The throbbing began to ease and became a warmth that spread throughout her and centred on her groin. Her wriggling continued but became a movement of her hips; a frustrated, desperate for sex sort of wriggle.

"It looks like she's ready for her initiation." Sharon opened eyes that she didn't even know where closed, to see Aaron looking down at her naked, highly aroused body. "Are you horny, sweetheart?"

"God yes!" The voice that came from her, didn't sound like hers. Sharon sounded like one of the bimbos in the nursery. "I need some cock so bad!"

Siobhan moved one of her hands down from Sharon's tits to make circles around her clitoris. "She's absolutely soaking darling," she told her husband. "Better get your cock inside her fast!"

There was no question in anyone's mind that Aaron was going to fuck this sexy young woman; the same woman his elderly father had recently been inside. Certainly, Sharon had no doubts. Siobhan eased her ankles out of the stirrups and pushed her legs even wider apart as her husband unzipped a very hard and very substantial cock. He took Sharon by the legs and tugged her suddenly down the couch until her sopping wet cunt almost slipped straight on to him. Then he leant forward to complete the motion, spearing her all the way in one go.

Sharon had always loved sex and generally came very quickly with a cock inside her. This was different though. The pleasure she was getting from this shaft of meat sawing in and out of her pussy was out of this world. It was almost transcendental and at that time it became her everything. She couldn't imagine being anywhere else than on Aaron's magnificent cock.

She had another growing desire though. "Please suck my boobies," she whined in an unfamiliar baby voice. "Pleeeease!"

"I've got this!" Siobhan was still in her doctor's coat. She leant over and sucked a long rubbery nipple into her mouth.

Over the next ten minutes or so, Sharon lost count of the number of orgasms that wracked her sensitive body. Her pussy convulsed and clamped around her Master while her nipples pumped what seemed to be endless pints of milk into her Mistress's hungry mouth.

Aaron finally erupted inside his new dairy cow, forcing so much cum into her womb that it poured out when he withdrew. Siobhan had a big smile on her face and milk all over her perfect face. "Oh my God Aaron, you've got to taste her. She's producing gold top!"

Aaron tasted the milk on his wife's lips, passionately snogging her as Sharon's juices dried on his cock. "She's gonna be a great addition to the herd."

"Come on," Siobhan pulled the young woman to her feet. "Let's get you settled in with the other girls." Sharon followed her Mistress meekly, eyes full of wonder; spunk running down her leg and milk still leaking from her nipples.

"Better start her off with a hose down," Aaron called after them.

ABOUT THE AUTHOR

A suburban Mum by day and who likes to let her hair down at night. Either blessed or cursed with a high sex drive, Charlotte is lucky to have a fantastic husband who looks after her in every respect but also allows her to research all aspects of her writing. She loves to write about sexy submissive ladies because at heart that's what she is. She writes about her girls being put into often extreme and difficult circumstances by strong men who care about them and ultimately ensure they are loved and looked after. She writes what she likes to read and it appeals to men and women alike.

CPSIA information can be obtained
at www.ICGtesting.com
Printed in the USA
LVHW051411270921
698830LV00030B/2314